GIRL MEETS BOY

Ali Smith

CANONGATE

Edinburgh · London · New York · Melbourne

First published in Great Britain in 2007 by
Canongate Books Ltd, 14 High Street,
Edinburgh EH1 1TE

This paperback edition first published in 2008
by Canongate Books

3

British Library Cataloguing-in-Publication Data
A catalogue record for this book is available on
request from the British Library

UK paperback
ISBN 978 1 84767 068 7

Export paperback
ISBN 978 1 84767 227 8

Typeset in Van Dijck by
Palimpsest Book Production Ltd, Grangemouth, Stirlingshire

Printed and bound in Great Britain by Clays Ltd, St Ives plc

www.canongate.net

Myths are universal and timeless stories that reflect and shape our lives – they explore our desires, our fears, our longings and provide narratives that remind us what it means to be human. *The Myths* series brings together some of the world's finest writers, each of whom has retold a myth in a contemporary and memorable way. Authors in the series include: Chinua Achebe, Alai, Karen Armstrong, Margaret Atwood, AS Byatt, Michel Faber, David Grossman, Milton Hatoum, Natsuo Kirino, Alexander McCall Smith, Tomás Eloy Martínez, Klas Östergren, Victor Pelevin, Ali Smith, Donna Tartt, Su Tong, Dubravka Ugresic, Salley Vickers and Jeanette Winterson.

Τάδε νυν ἑταίραις
ταῖς εμαισι τέρπνα κάλως ἀείσω.

for Lucy Cuthbertson

for Sarah Wood

Far away, in some other category, far
away from the snobbery and glitter in
which our souls and bodies have been
entangled, is forged the instrument
of the new dawn.
E M Forster

It is the mark of a narrow world that
it mistrusts the undefined.
Joseph Roth

I am thinking about the difference
between history and myth. Or between
expression and vision. The need for
narrative and the simultaneous need
to escape the prison-house of the
story — to misquote.
Kathy Acker

Gender ought not to be construed as
a stable identity . . . rather, gender is an
identity tenuously constituted in time.
Judith Butler

Practise only impossibilities.
John Lyly

I

Let me tell you about when I was a girl, our grandfather says.

It is Saturday evening; we always stay at their house on Saturdays. The couch and the chairs are shoved back against the walls. The teak coffee table from the middle of the room is up under the window. The floor has been cleared for the backward and forward somersaults, the juggling with oranges and eggs, the how-to-do-a-cart-wheel, how-to-stand-on-your-head, how-to-walk-on-your-hands lessons. Our grandfather holds us upside-down by the legs until we get our balance. Our grandfather worked in a circus before he met and married our grandmother. He once did headstands on top of a whole troupe of headstanders. He once walked a tightrope across the Thames. The Thames is a river in London, which is five hundred and twenty-seven miles from here, according to the mileage chart in the RAC book in among our father's books at home. Oh, across

the Thames, was it? our grandmother says. Not across
the falls at Niagara? Ah, Niagara, our grandfather says.
Now that was a whole other kittle of fish.

It is after gymnastics and it is before Blind Date.
Sometimes after gymnastics it is The Generation
Game instead. Back in history The Generation Game
was our mother's favourite programme, way before we
were born, when she was as small as us. But our
mother isn't here any more, and anyway we prefer
Blind Date, where every week without fail a boy
chooses a girl from three girls and a girl chooses a boy
from three boys, with a screen and Cilla Black in
between them each time. Then the chosen boys and
girls from last week's programme come back and talk
about their blind date, which has usually been awful,
and there is always excitement about whether there'll
be a wedding, which is what it's called before people
get divorced, and to which Cilla Black will get to
wear a hat.

But which is Cilla Black, then, boy or girl? She doesn't
seem to be either. She can look at the boys if she wants;
she can go round the screen and look at the girls. She
can go between the two sides of things like a magician,

or a joke. The audience always laughs with delight when she does it.

You're being ridiculous, Anthea, Midge says shrugging her eyes at me.

Cilla Black is from the sixties, our grandmother says as if that explains everything.

It is Saturday tea-time, after supper and before our bath. It is always exciting to sit in the chairs in the places they usually aren't. Midge and I, one on each knee, are on our grandfather's lap and all three of us are wedged into the pushed-back armchair waiting for our grandmother to settle. She drags her own armchair closer to the electric fire. She puts her whole weight behind the coffee table and shoves it over so she can watch the football results. You don't need the sound up for that. Then she neatens the magazines on the under-rack of the table and then she sits down. Steam rises off teacups. We've got the taste of buttered toast in our mouths. At least, I assume we all have it, since we've all been eating the same toast, well, different bits of the same toast. Then I start to worry. Because what if we all taste things differently? What if each bit of toast tastes completely different? After all, the two bits

I've eaten definitely tasted a bit different even from each other. I look round the room, from head to head of each of us. Then I taste the taste in my own mouth again.

So did I never tell you about the time they put me in jail for a week when I was a girl? our grandfather says.

What for? I say.

For saying you were a girl when you weren't one, Midge says.

For writing words, our grandfather says.

What words? I say.

NO VOTES NO GOLF, our grandfather says. They put us in jail because we wrote it into the golf green with acid, me and my friend. What's a young girl like you wanting acid for? the chemist asked me when I went to get it.

Grandad, stop it, Midge says.

What's a girl like you wanting with fifteen bottles of it? he said. I told him the truth, more fool me. I want to write words on the golf course with it, I told him and he sold me it, right enough, but then he went and told Harry Cathcart at the police station exactly who'd been round buying a job lot of acid. We were proud to

go to jail, though. I was proud when they came to get
me. I said to them all at the police station, I'm doing
this because my mother can't write her name with
words, never mind vote. Your great-grandmother wrote
her name with Xs. X X X. Mary Isobel Gunn. And
when we went on the Mud March, our grandfather says.
Boy oh boy. It was called the Mud March because —
because why?

Because of some mud, I say.

Because of the mud we got all up the hems of our
skirts, our grandfather says.

Grandad, Midge says. Don't.

You should've heard the mix of accents coming out of
us all, it was like a huge flock of all the different birds,
all in the sky, all singing at once. Blackbirds and
chaffinches and seagulls and thrushes and starlings and
swifts and peewits, imagine. From all over the country
we came, from Manchester, Birmingham, Liverpool,
Huddersfield, Leeds, all the girls that worked in cloth-
ing, because that's what most of us did, textiles I mean,
and from Glasgow, from Fife, even from right up here
we went. Soon they were so afraid of us marching that
they made brand new laws against us. They said we

could only march in groups of no more than twelve of us. And each group of twelve girls had to be fifty yards away from any other group of twelve. And what do you think they threw at us for marching, what do you think they threw at us when we spoke in front of the great hordes of listening people?

Eggs and oranges, I say. Mud.

Tomatoes and fishheads, Midge says.

And what did we throw at the Treasury, at the Home Office, at the Houses of Parliament? he says.

Fishheads, I say.

I am finding the idea of throwing fishheads at official historic buildings very funny. Our grandfather tightens his hold round me.

No, he says. Stones, to break the windows.

Not very ladylike, Midge says from the other side of his head.

Actually, Miss Midge —, our grandfather says.

My name's not Midge, Midge says.

Actually, as it happens, we were very ladylike indeed. We threw the stones in little linen bags that we'd made ourselves with our own hands especially to put the stones in. That's how ladylike we were. But never mind

that. Never mind that. Listen to this. Are you listening?
Are you ready?

Here we go, our grandmother says.

Did I never tell you about the time when I was a
really important, couldn't-be-done-without part of the
smuggling-out-of-the-country of Burning Lily herself,
the famous Building-Burning-Girl of the North East?

No, I say.

No, Midge says.

Well, I will then. Will I? our grandfather says.

Yes, I say.

Okay, Midge says.

Are you sure? he says.

Yes! we say together.

Burning Lily, he says, was famous. She was famous for
lots of things. She was a dancer, and she was very very
beautiful.

Always the eye for the lasses, our grandmother says
with her own eyes on the television.

And one day, our grandfather says, on her twenty-
first birthday, the day that the beautiful (though not
near as beautiful as your grandmother, obviously) the
day that the beautiful Burning Lily became a fully

– 9 –

fledged grown-up – which is what's supposed to happen on the day you're twenty-one – she looked in the mirror and said to herself, I've had enough of this. I'm going to change things. So she went straight out and broke a window as a birthday present to herself.

Ridiculous present, Midge says. I'm asking for a Mini Cooper for mine.

But soon she decided that breaking windows, though it was a good start, wasn't quite enough. So she started setting fire to buildings – buildings that didn't have any people in them. That worked. That got their attention. She was always being carted off to jail then. And in there, in jail, in her cell, you know what she did?

What? Midge says.

She just stopped eating, he says.

Why? I say and as I say it I taste the toast taste again all through the inside of me.

Because she was like anorexic, Midge says, and had seen too many pictures of herself in magazines.

Because there wasn't anything else for her to do, our grandfather says to me over the top of Midge's head. They all did it, to protest, then. We'd all have done it. I'd have done it too. So would you.

Well *I* wouldn't, Midge says.

Yes you would. You'd do it too, if it was the only thing you could do. So then they made Burning Lily eat.

How? I said. You can't *make* someone eat.

By putting a tube down her throat and by putting food down the tube. Except, they put it down the wrong part of her throat, into her windpipe, by mistake, and they pumped food right into her lungs.

Why? I say.

Uch, Midge says.

Rob, our grandmother says.

They have to know, our grandfather says. It's true. It happened. And that thing with putting the tube into her windpipe had made her very very ill, so they had to let her out of the jail because she nearly died. And that would have been very bad publicity for the police and the jail and the government. But by the time Burning Lily got better they'd passed a new law which said: As soon as one of those girls has made herself better out there, and isn't going to die here in jail, on our hands, as if it was us who killed her, we can go straight back out and arrest her again.

But you know what?

What? I say.

What? Midge says.

Burning Lily kept on slipping through their fingers.
She kept on getting away with it. She kept on setting
fire to the empty buildings.

She was like a lunatic, Midge says.

Only empty buildings, mind, our grandfather says. *I
will never endanger any human life except my own*, she said. *I
always call out when I go into the building to make sure no one
is in it. But I will carry on doing it for as long as it takes to
change things for the better*. That's what she said in court.
She used lots of different names in court. Lilian. Ida.
May. It was before they knew what everyone looked
like, like they do today, so she could slip through their
fingers like water does if you clench your fist round it.
It was before they used film and photos like they do
now, to know who everyone is.

I hold up my hand, in a fist. I open it, then close
it.

And she kept on doing it, he says. And the police
were always after her. And next time, we knew, she'd
surely die, she would die if they got her again, because

she was too weak to do that starving thing many more times. And one day, now, are you listening?

Yes, we say.

One day, our grandfather says, one of our friends came round to my house and told me: Tomorrow you've got to dress up as a message boy.

What's a message boy? I say.

Shh, Midge says.

I was small, our grandfather says, I was nineteen, but I could pass for twelve or thirteen. And I looked a bit like a boy.

Yeah, Midge says, cause you *were* one.

Shh, I say.

And I checked through the clothes she'd brought me in the bag, our grandfather says, they were pretty clean, they didn't smell too bad, they smelt a bit leathery, a bit of the smell of boys.

Uch, Midge says.

What's the smell of boys? I say.

And it looked likely that they'd fit me. And lo and behold, they did. So I put them on the next morning, and I got into the grocer's van that stopped for me outside the door. And the girl driving the truck got out, and a boy took over the wheel, and she gave the boy a kiss as she got out. And before she got into the back of the van in under the canvas the girl gave me a rolled-up comic and an apple, and a basket of things, tea, sugar, a cabbage, some carrots. And she said, pull your cap down low and put your head inside the comic now, and start eating at that apple when you get out of the van. So I did those things, I did what she said, I opened the comic at random and held it up in front of me, and the pictures juggled up and down in front of my eyes all the way there, and when we got to the right house the boy driving stopped the van, and the front door of the house opened, and a woman shouted, All right! It's here! And I went round the back, that's where message boys were supposed to go, I was down behind the comic, and I took two bites out of the apple, which was a big one, apples were a lot bigger then, back in the days when I was a girl.

This time Midge doesn't say anything. She is completely listening, like I am.

And in the corridor of the big old house I saw myself in a mirror, except it wasn't a mirror, and it wasn't me. It was someone else dressed exactly the same, it was a fine-looking boy wearing the exact same clothes. But he was very very handsome, and that was how I knew he wasn't me and I wasn't him.

Rob, our grandmother says.

He was handsome, though he was very thin and pale, and he gave me a great big smile. And the woman who'd taken me through the house, she upended the basket so the groceries fell out all over her floor, like she couldn't care less about groceries, and then she handed the empty basket to the handsome boy and she told me to give him the comic and the apple. He slung the basket lightly on his arm and let the comic fall open in his hand, then he took a bite himself out of the apple in his other hand, and as he went out the door he turned and winked at me. And I saw. It wasn't a boy at all. It was a beautiful girl. It was beautiful Burning Lily herself, dressed just like I was, who'd turned and winked at me then.

Our grandfather winks over at our grandmother. Eh, Helen? he says.

Way back in the Celtic tribes, our grandmother says, women had the franchise. You always have to fight to get the thing you've lost. Even though you maybe don't

know you ever had it in the first place. She turns back
to the television. Christ. Six nil, she says. She shakes
her head.

I want the French eyes, I say.

You've got all the eyes you need, our grandfather
says, thanks to girls like Burning Lily. And you know
what, you know what? She got as far as the coast that
day, miles and miles all the way to a waiting boat, without the police who were watching the house even knowing she'd been and she'd gone.

Grandad, you're like insane, Midge says. Because if
you work it out, even if you *were* a girl, that story
would make you born right at the beginning of the
century, and yeah, I mean, you're old and everything,
but you're not that old.

Midge, my sweet fierce cynical heart, our grandfather
says. You're going to have to learn the kind of hope
that makes things history. Otherwise there'll be no good
hope for your own grand truths and no good truths for
your own grandchildren.

My name's Imogen, Midge says and gets down off his
knee.

Our grandmother stands up.

Your grandfather likes to think that all the stories in the world are his to tell, she says.

Just the important ones, our grandfather says. Just the ones that need the telling. Some stories always need telling more than others. Right, Anthea?

Right, Grandad, I say.

Yeah, right, Midge had said. And then you went straight outside and threw a stone at the kitchen window, do you remember that?

She pointed at the window, the one right there in front of us now, with its vase of daffodils and its curtains that she'd gone all the way to Aberdeen to get.

No, I said. I don't remember that at all. I don't remember any of it. All I remember is something about Blind Date and there always being toast.

We both stared at the window. It was the same window, but different, obviously, nearly fifteen years different. It didn't look like it could ever have been broken, or ever have been any different to how it was right now.

Did it break? I said.

Yeah, it broke, she said. Of course it broke. That's

the kind of girl you were. I should have told them to put it into your Pure psychology report. Highly suggestible. Blindly rebellious.

Ha, I said. Hardly. I'm not the suggestible one. I nodded my head towards the front of the house. I mean, who went and bought a motorbike for thousands of pounds because it's got the word REBEL painted on it? I said.

That's not why I bought it, Midge said and her neck up to her ears went as red as the bike. It was the right price and the right shape, she said. I didn't buy it because of any stupid word on it.

I began to feel bad about what I'd said. I felt bad as soon as it came out of my mouth. Words. Look what they can do. Because now maybe she wouldn't be able to get on that bike in the same innocent way ever again and it would be my fault. I'd maybe ruined her bike for her. I'd definitely annoyed her, I knew by the way she pulled rank on me with such calm, told me I'd better not be late, and told me not to call her Midge at work, especially not in front of Keith. Then she clicked the front door shut behind her with a quietness that was an affront.

I tried to remember which one at Pure Keith was.
They all looked the same, the bosses with their slightly
Anglified accents and their trendily close-shaved heads.
They all looked far too old for haircuts like that. They
all looked nearly bald. They all looked like they were
maybe called Keith.

I heard her taking the cover off and folding it neatly,
then I heard her get on the bike, start it up and roar
out of the drive.

Rebel.

It was raining. I hoped she'd go easy in the rain. I
hoped her brakes were good. It had rained every day
here since I'd got back, all eight days. Scottish rain's no
myth, it's real all right. I ain't got nothing but rain,
baby, eight days a week. The rain it raineth every day.
When that I was and a little tiny girl, with a hey, ho,
the wind and the rain.

Yes, because that was another thing that made Midge
furious when we were little tiny girls, that he was
always changing the words to things. If you can keep
your head when all about you. Are losing theirs and
blaming it on you. If you can bear to hear the truth
you've spoken. If you can force your heart and nerve

and sinew. If you can fill the unforgiving minute. With sixty seconds' worth of distance run. Yours is the earth and everything that's in it. And – which is more – you'll be a woman, my daughter NO NO NO GRANDAD IT DOESN'T RHYME she used to squeal, she used to stand on the linoleum right there, where the new parquet was now, and shout in a kind of amazing rage, don't change it! you're changing it! it isn't right! it's wrong! I had forgotten that too. Amazing rage, how sweet the sound. And *Midge, can I have that book? You can if you say the magic word, what's the magic word?* Imogen was the magic word. *Midge, can I finish your chips? Midge, can I borrow your bike? Midge, will you say it was you who broke it? I will if you say the magic word, what's the magic word?* Something about Midge had changed. Something fundamental. I tried to think what it was. It was right in front of my eyes and yet I couldn't quite see it.

They'd had a teak coffee table. I remembered now how proud they'd been about it being made of teak. God knows why. Was teak such a big deal? The teak coffee table was long gone. All their things had gone. I had no idea where. The only real sense of the two of them still here came from the way the light fell through the same glass of the front door, and the framed photo Midge'd put on the wall next to where the dinette door used to be.

Dinette. What a word. What a long-gone word, a word sunk to the bottom of the sea. Midge had knocked through the walls of the dinette into the living room to make one huge room. She had had central heating put in. She'd knocked through from the bathroom into the littlest bedroom where I used to sleep on the Saturday nights we stayed here, to make a bigger bathroom; now there was a bath where my single bed had been. She'd tarmacked over the front garden where our grandmother used to have her roses and her pinks. Now Midge's bike was kept there.

They looked old in the photo, I could see that now. They looked like two old people. Their features were soft. He looked smooth, sweet-faced, almost girlish. She looked strong, clear-boned, like a smiling young man from some Second World War film had climbed inside an older skin. They looked wise. They looked like people who didn't mind, who were wise to how little time was left. Come in boat number two, your time is up. Five

years ago they went on holiday to Devon. They bought
a trimaran at a boating shop on a whim, and they sent
our father a note. Dear son, gone to see the world, love
to the girls, back soon. They sailed off on their whim.
They'd never been sailing in their lives.

Wise fools. They'd sent us postcards from the coasts of
Spain and Portugal. Then the postcards stopped. Two
years ago our father came up north and put up a head-
stone in the cemetery above their empty plot, the plot
they bought before we were born, with their names and a
photo on it, the same photo I was looking at now, and the
words on the stone under the trees, next to the canal, in
among the birdsong and the hundreds of other stones,
above the empty square of earth, were ROBERT AND
HELEN GUNN   BELOVED PARENTS AND
GRANDPARENTS   LOST AT SEA   2003.

On the backs of the dolphins. Acquainted with the
waves.

Then he gave the house to us, if we wanted it.
Midge moved in. Now I was here too, thanks to Midge.
Now I had a job too, thanks to Midge.

I didn't particularly want to be thankful to Midge.

But I was home, I had a home here in Inverness,

thanks to Midge. Well, thanks to the two of *them*, full
fathom five, seaweed swaying round their unbound
bones shifting on the sand of the seabed. Was the
seabed dark? Was it cold? Did any light get down there
from the sun? They'd been kidnapped by sirens,
ensnared by Scylla and Charybdis. Cilla and Charybdis.
That was what had got me thinking about Blind Date.
That was why I'd remembered what little I hadn't
completely forgotten of those Saturdays, the Saturday
toast, the Saturday television. That, and the fixed and
fluid features on the wall, of the old, the wise.

I wished I was old. I was tired of being so young, so
stupidly knowing, so stupidly forgetful. I was tired of
having to be anything at all. I felt like the Internet, full
of every kind of information but none of it mattering
more than any of it, and all of its little links like thin
white roots on a broken plant dug out of the soil, lying
drying on its side. And whenever I tried to access
myself, whenever I'd try to click on me, try to go any
deeper when it came to the meaning of 'I', I mean
deeper than a single fast-loading page on Facebook or
MySpace, it was as if I knew that one morning I'd wake
up and try to log on to find that not even *that* version

of 'I' existed any more, because the servers all over the world were all down. And that's how rootless. And that's how fragile. And what would poor Anthea do then, poor thing?

I'd sit in a barn. And keep myself warm. And hide my head under my wing, poor thing.

I wondered if Midge would remember that song, about the bird in the barn and the snow coming. I remembered it as something to do with our mother. I didn't know if that was a true memory or if I'd just made it up.

I sat down on the kitchen floor. I traced a square in the parquet with my finger. Come on. Get a grip. I should have been on my way to work. I should have been on my way to my next new day at the new Pure. I had a good new job. I would be making good money. It was all good. I was a Creative. That's what I was. That's who I was. Anthea Gunn, Pure Creative.

But I stared at my grandparents in their photo, with their arms round each other and their heads together, and I wished that my own bones were unbound, I wished they were mingling, picked clean by fish, with the bones of another body, a body my bones

and heart and soul had loved with unfathomable
certainty for decades, and both of us down deep now,
lost to everything but the fact of bare bones on a dark
seabed.

Midge was right. I was going to be late for work. I
was late already.

Not Midge. Imogen. (Keith.) (What's the magic
word?)

At least my sister had a Shakespearian name. At least
her name meant something. Anthea. For God's sake.

Weren't people supposed to get named after gods and
goddesses, rivers, places that mattered, the heroines of
books or plays, or members of their family who'd gone
before them?

I went upstairs and put on the right kind of clothes.
I came downstairs. I got my umbrella. I put my jacket
on. I stopped and looked in the mirror on my way out
the front door. I was twenty-one years old. My hair was
light and my eyes were blue. I was Anthea Gunn,
named after some girl from the past I'd never seen, a
girl on a Saturday evening tv show who always gave
things a twirl, who always wore pretty frocks, and
whom my mother, when she herself was a little tiny

girl, had longed with all her heart to be like when she finally grew up.

I went outside mournful, and I hit pure air. The air was full of birdsong. I went outside expecting rain but it was sunny, it was so suddenly so openly sunny, with so sharp a spring light coming off the river, that I went down the side of the riverbank and sat in among the daffodils.

People went past on the pavement above. They looked down at me like I was mad. A seagull patrolled the railing. It eyed me like I was mad.

Clearly nobody ever went down the riverbank. Clearly nobody was supposed to.

I slid myself down to the water's edge. I was wearing the wrong kind of shoes to do it. I took them off. The grass was very wet. The soles of my tights went dark with it. I'd be ruining my work clothes.

There was blossom on the surface of the Ness, close to the bank, lapping near my feet, a thin rime of floating petals that had blown off the trees under the cathedral behind me. The river was lined with churches, as if to prove that decent people still

believed in things. Maybe they did. Maybe they
thought it made a difference, all the ritual marryings
and christenings and confirmings and funereals, all the
centuries of asking, in their different churches each
filled with the same cold air off the mountains and the
Firth, for things to reveal themselves as having meaning after all, for some proof the world was held in
larger hands than human hands. I'd be happy, myself, I
thought as I sat in the wet grass with my hands in the
warmth still inside my shoes, just to know that the
world was a berry in the beak of a bird, or was nothing
more than a slab of sloped grassy turf like this, fished
out of cosmic nothingness one beautiful spring morning by some meaningless creature or other. That would
do. That would do fine. It would be fine, just to know
that for sure.

The river itself was fast and black. It was comforting.
It had been here way before any town with its shops, its
churches, its restaurants, its houses, its townspeople
with all their comings and goings, its boatbuilding, its
fishing, its port, its years of wars over who got the
money from these, then its shipping of Highland boy
soldiers down south for Queen Victoria's wars, in boats

on the brand new canal then all along the lochs in the ice-cut crevasse of the Great Glen.

I could, if I chose, just walk into the river. I could stand up and let myself fall the whole slant of the bank. I could just let the fast old river have me, toss myself in like a stone.

There was a stone by my foot. It was a local stone, a white-ridged stone with a glint of mica through it. I threw it in instead.

The river laughed. I swear it did. It laughed and it changed as I watched. As it changed, it stayed the same. The river was all about time, it was about how little time actually mattered. I looked at my watch. Fuck. I was an hour and a half late. Ha ha! The river laughed at me again.

So I laughed too, and instead of going to work I went into town to hang out at the new shopping centre for a while.

We had all the same shops here now as in every big city. They had all the big brands and all the same labels. That made us, up here, every bit as good as all the big cities all over the country – whatever 'good' meant.

But the shopping centre was full of people shopping who looked immensely sad, and the people working in the shops there looked even sadder, and some of them looked mean, looked at me as if I was a threat, as if I might steal things, wandering round not buying anything at half past ten in the morning. So I left the new mall and went to the second-hand bookshop instead.

The second-hand bookshop used to be a church. Now it was a church for books. But there were only so many copies of other people's given-away books that you could thumb through without getting a bit nauseous. Like that poem I knew, about how you sit and read your way through a book then close the book and put it on the shelf, and maybe, life being so short, you'll die before you ever open that book again and its pages, the single pages, shut in the book on the shelf, will maybe never see light again, which is why I had to leave the shop, because the man who owned it was looking at me oddly, because I was doing the thing I find myself doing in all bookshops because of that maddening poem – taking a book off a shelf and fanning it open so that each page sees some light, then putting it back on, then taking the next one along off and doing the same, which is very time-consuming, though they don't seem to mind as much in second-hand shops as they do in Borders and Waterstones etc, where they tend not to like it if you bend or break the spines on new books.

Then I stopped to have a look at the big flat stone cemented into the pavement outside the Town House, the famous stone, the oldest most important stone in town, the oldest proof of itself as a town that the town I grew up in had. It was reputedly the stone the washerwomen used to rest their baskets of clothes on, on their way to and from the river, or the stone they used to scrub their clothes against when they were washing them, I didn't know which was true, or if either of those was true.

My mobile was going off in my pocket and because, without looking, I knew it would be Pure, and because I thought for a moment of Midge, I decided to be a good girl, whatever good means, and I made for Pure instead, up the hill, past the big billboard, the one that someone had very prettily defaced.

Matchmake.com. Get What You Want. In smaller writing at the bottom, *Get What You Want In The First Six Weeks or Get Six Months' Free Membership.*

It was a massive pink poster with little cartoon people drawn on it in couples standing outside little houses, a bit like weather people. They didn't have faces, they had cartoon blank circles instead, but they were wearing uniforms or outfits and holding things to make it clearer what they were. A nurse (female) and a policeman (male). That was one couple. A sailor (male) and a pole-dancer (female). A teacher (female) and a doctor (male). An executive (male) and an arty-looking person (female). A dustman (male) and a ballet dancer (female). A pirate (male) and a person holding a baby (female). A cook (female) and a truck driver (male). The difference between male and female was breasts and hair.

Underneath the Get What You Want line someone had written, in red paint, in fine calligraphic hand: DON'T BE STUPID. MONEY WON'T BUY IT.

Then, below, in a kind of graffiti signature, the strange word: IPHISOL.

Iphisol.

You're late, Becky on Reception said as I went past. Careful. They're looking for you.

I thanked her. I took off my coat and hung it up. I

sat down. I switched my computer on. I got Google up. I typed the strange word in and I clicked on Search: the web.

Well done, Anthea, on finally getting in, one of the shaveys said behind me.

In what? I said.

In to work, Anthea, he said. He leaned in over my shoulder. His breath smelt of coffee and badness. I moved my head away. He was holding one of the customised plastic coffee tubs with the clip-on tops. It said Pure on it.

I'm being sarcastic, Anthea, he said.

Right, I said. I wished I could remember his name so I could use it all the time like he was using mine.

Everybody else managed to get here by nine all right, he said. Even the girls doing work experience from the High School. They were on time. Becky on Reception. She was on time. I won't even bring your sister into this as a comparison, Anthea.

Good of you, I said.

The shavey flinched slightly in case I was daring to answer back.

I'm just wondering what could have caused you not

to be able to meet the same standards everybody else manages to meet. Any idea, Anthea?

Your search – iphisol – did not match any documents. Suggestions: Make sure all words are spelled correctly. Try different keywords. Try more general keywords.

I've been working quite hard on the concept, I said. But I had to do it off-site. My apologies. I'm really sorry, eh, Brian.

Uh huh, he said. Well, we're waiting for you. The whole Creatives group has been waiting for you for most of the morning, including Keith. You know the pressure Keith's under when it comes to time.

Why did you wait? I asked. Why did you not just go ahead? I wouldn't have minded. I'd not have been offended.

Boardroom two, he said. Five minutes. Okay Anthea?

Okay Brian, I said.

He *was* called Brian. Thank you, gods. Or if he wasn't, he didn't complain, or didn't give a fuck what I was saying, or maybe wasn't actually listening to anything I said.

★　★　★

Okay, ladies and gents, Keith said. (Keith sounded American. I'd not yet met Keith. Keith was the boss of bosses.) Let's do it. Get the lights, ah, ah, Imogen? Good girl. Thank you.

Midge wasn't speaking to me. She'd ignored me when I'd come into the room.

I want you to look at these slides, Keith said. And I want you to look at them in silence.

We did as we were told.

Eilean Donan Castle on a cloudy day. The clouds reflecting in the water round the castle.

The old bridge at Carrbridge on a snowy day. A ridge of snow on the bridge. The water under it reflecting the blue of the sky. Ice at its edges.

A whale's back rising out of very blue water.

An archaeological site with a stretch of blue water beyond it.

A loch in a green treeless valley with a war memorial at the front of it.

An island rising out of very blue water.

A Highland cow in an autumnal setting, behind it a thin line of light on water.

The town. The river I'd just thrown a stone into,

running right through the centre of it. The sky, the elegant bridges, the river banks, the buildings on the banks, their shimmering second selves standing on their heads in their reflections.

Team, Keith said in the dark. Thank you all for being here. Water is history. Water is mystery. Water is nature. Water is life. Water is archaeology. Water is civilisation. Water is where we live. Water is here and water is now. Get the message. Get it in a bottle. Water in a bottle makes two billion pounds a year in the UK alone. Water in a bottle costs the consumer roughly ten thousand times the amount that the same measure of tapwater costs him. Water is everything we imagine at Pure. The Pure imagination. That's my theme today. So here's my question. How, precisely, do we bottle the imagination?

One of the shaveys shifted in his chair as if to answer. Keith held a hand up to quieten him.

Ten years ago, Keith said, there were twenty-eight countries in the world with not enough water. In less than twenty years' time, the number of countries which don't have enough water will have doubled. In less than twenty years' time, over eight hundred million people – that's right, eight hundred million people, people very much, in their way, exactly like you or me – will be living without access to enough water. Lights, please. Thanks.

The picture of our town on the screen paled. Keith was sitting up on the desk at the end of the room with his legs crossed like a Buddha. He looked down at us all. Though I'd only been working here for half a week I'd heard rumours about these meetings. Becky on Reception had told me about them. The phones had to be muted for them. One of the High School girls had mentioned them, how weird it was when the Tuesday Creative Lecture was over and everybody came out as if hypnotised, or wounded. That's what she called it, the Tuesday Creative Lecture. Keith, she'd told me, flew over for these meetings specially. He flew in every Monday, then out again after every Tuesday Creative Lecture.

I felt suddenly sick. I'd been late for the Tuesday Creative Lecture. Maybe the boss of bosses would be late for his outward flight because of me.

That's why Pure's here, Keith was saying. That's why Pure is branching into water subsidiary, that's why Pure is investing such a wealth of international finance and promise into such a small locality. Team, fresh water. The world is running out of it. Forty per cent of all the world's freshwater rivers and streams are now too polluted for human use or consumption. Think about what that really means.

He drew himself up, his back straight, suddenly silent. Everyone in the room sat forward, pencils and Palm Pilots at the ready. I felt myself sitting forward too. I didn't know why. He held his hands up in the air for a moment, as if to stop time. Then he spoke.

What it means is that water is the perfect commodity. Because water is running out. There will never, ever, ever again, not be an urgent need for water. So how will we do it? Question one. How will we bottle our Highland oil? Question two. What will we call it? Question three. What shape will its bottles be? Question four. What will it say on the labels on the bottles? And finally, question five. Will it say anything on the lids of the bottles? Answers, team! Answers!

All round me there was frantic scribbling down, there were little clickings of buttons. Keith got down off the desk. He began to walk back and fore at the top of the room.

What you come up with, he said, will need to indi-
cate that water really matters to us. It will need to let
us know that human beings aren't ruled by nature, that
on the contrary, they ARE nature. That's good. They
ARE nature. It will need to be about mindset. It will
need not just to open minds to our product, but to
suggest that our product is the most open-minded on
the market. We can't use Purely. The Alaskans use
Purely. We can't use Clearly. The Canadians use Clearly.
We can't use Highland. Our biggest rivals use Highland.
But our name will need to imply all three. So come on,
people. Throw me a name. I need a name. We need a
name for our water. Come on. Ideas. I need to hear
them. Purely. Clearly. Highland. Nature. Power. Ideas.
Now. Concepts. Now.

Keith snapped his fingers as he said each single word.

Fluidity, a nice shavey called out next to me.
Recycling. How water is smart, how water is graceful,
how water, since it can change shape and form, can
make us versatile –

Good, Keith said, good, good! Keep it coming –

– and how we're all actually about seventy-five per
cent water. We need to suggest that water IS us. We

need to suggest that water can unite us. No matter what our political or national differences.

That's very, very good, Keith said. Well done, Paul. Run with it.

The whole room turned and bristled with jealousy at Paul.

Of the first water, the one who was maybe called Brian said. Still waters run deep, a shavey called Dominic shouted from across the room. Soon the room was running pretty deep in thesaurus clichés. In deep water. Won't hold water. Get into hot water. Head above water. Throw cold water.

Water is about well-being, Midge said. About being well.

Nobody heard her.

It's all about well-being, an unfamiliar Creative said on the other side of the room.

I like that, Keith said. Very good point, Norm.

I saw Midge look down, disheartened, and in that moment I saw what it was that was different about my sister now. I saw it in the turn of her head and the movement of her too-thin wrist. How had I not seen it? She was far too thin. She was really thin.

And product package will dwell on how water makes you healthy, keeps you healthy, Dominic said.

Maybe marketed with health-conscious products or a healthy make-yourself-over or let-yourself-relax package specifically aimed at women stroke families, Norm said. Water keeps your kids healthy.

Good point, Norm, Keith said.

I'd had enough.

You could call it Och Well, I said.

Call it – ? Keith said.

He stared at me.

The whole room turned and stared at me.

I'm dead, I thought. Och well.

You could call it Affluent, I said. That pretty much sums it up. Or maybe that sounds too like Effluent. I know. You could call it Main Stream. On the lid it could say You're Always Safer Sticking With The Main Stream.

The whole room was silent, and not in a good way.

You could call it Scottish Tap, I said into the hush. That'd be good and honest. Whatever good means.

Keith raised his eyebrows. He jutted out his chin.

Transparency, Midge said quick. It's not a bad route, Keith. It could be a really, really good route, no?

A we-won't-mess-with-you route, Paul said nodding. It's mindset all right. And it combines honesty and nationality in the same throw. Honest Scottishness. Honest-to-goodness goodness in a bottle.

It takes and makes a stand, Midge said. Doesn't it? And that's half the bottle, I mean battle.

Where you stand lets you know what really matters. If we suggest our bottled water takes and makes a stand, it'll become bottled idealism, Paul said.

Bottled identity, Midge said.

Bottled politics, Paul said.

I went to stand by the window where the water cooler was. I pressed the button and water bubbled out of the big plastic container into the little plastic cup. It tasted of plastic. I'm dead, I thought. That's that. It was a relief. The only thing I was sorry about was troubling Midge. She had been sweet there, trying to save me.

I watched a tiny bird fling itself through the air off the guttering above the Boardroom window and land on its feet on a branch of the tree over the huge Pure corporation sign at the front gate of the building. The bird's casual expertise pleased me. I wondered if that group of people outside, gathered at the front gate under the Pure sign, had seen it land.

They were standing there as if they were watching a play. Some were laughing. Some were gesticulating.

It was a lad, dressed for a wedding. He was up a ladder doing some kind of maintenance on the sign. The work experience girls from the school were watching him. So was Becky from Reception, some people who looked like passers-by, and one or two other people I recognised, people Midge had introduced me to, from Pure Press and Pure Personnel.

The nice shavey called Paul was standing beside me now at the water cooler. He nodded to me, apologetic, as he took a plastic cone and held it under the plastic tap. He looked grave. I was clearly going to be shot at dawn. Then he looked out of the window.

Something unorthodox seems to be happening at the Pure sign, he said.

When everybody in the Boardroom was round the window I slipped off to get my coat. I switched my computer off. I'd not yet put anything in the drawers of my desk so there was very little to take with me. I went past the empty reception, all the lights flashing like mad on the phones, and ran down the stairs and out into the sun.

It was a beautiful day.

The boy up the ladder at the gate was in a kilt and sporran. The kilt was a bright red tartan; the boy was black-waistcoated and had frilly cuffs, I could see the frills at his wrists as I came closer. I could see the glint of the knife in his sock. I could see the glint of the little diamond spangles on the waistcoat and the glint that came off the chain that held the sporran on. He had long dark hair winged with ringlets, like Johnny Depp in Pirates of the Caribbean, but cleaner. He was spray-painting, in beautiful red calligraphy, right under the Pure insignia, these words:

DON'T BE STUPID. WATER IS A HUMAN RIGHT. SELLING IT IN ANY WAY IS MORALLY WRO

The work experience girls were applauding and laughing. One of them was singing. Let the wind blow high, let the wind blow low. Through the streets in my kilt I'll go. All the lassies say hello. They saw me and waved at me. I waved back. A Press person was on a mobile. The rest of Press and Personnel were crowded

round looking concerned. Two security men stood list-
lessly at the foot of the ladder. One of them pointed
towards the building; I looked up, but its windows,
including the window I had myself been staring through
a minute ago, were the kind you can't see into.

I wondered if my sister was watching me from up
there. I had an urge to wave.

NG., the boy wrote.

The security men shook their heads at each other.

Becky from Reception winked at me then nodded,
serious-faced, at the security men. We watched the
long-limbed boy sign off, with a series of arrogant and
expert slants and curlicues, the final word at the
bottom of his handiwork:

IPHISOL.

He shook the paintcan, listened to the rattle it made,
thought about whether to keep it or to chuck it away,
then tucked it into the pocket of his waistcoat. He took
hold of the sides of the ladder, lifted his feet off the
rung in one move, put them on the outsides of the
downstruts and slid himself neatly to the ground. He
landed on his feet and he turned round.

My head, something happened to its insides. It was

as if a storm at sea happened, but only for a moment, and only on the inside of my head. My ribcage, something definitely happened there. It was as if it unknotted itself from itself, like the hull of a ship hitting rock, giving way, and the ship that I was opened wide inside me and in came the ocean.

He was the most beautiful boy I had ever seen in my life.

But he looked really like a girl.

She was the most beautiful boy I had ever seen in my life.

you

(Oh my God my sister is A GAY.)

(I am not upset. I am not upset. I am not upset. I am not upset.)

I am putting on my Stella McCartney Adidas tracksuit bottoms. I am lacing up my Nike runners. I am zipping up my Stella McCartney Adidas tracksuit top. I am going out the front door like I am a (normal) person just going out of a (normal) front door on a (normal) early summer day in the month of May and I am going for a run which is the kind of (normal) thing (normal) people do all the time.

There. I'm running. That feels better. I can feel the road beneath my feet. There. There. There.

(It is our mother's fault for splitting up with our father.)

(But if that's true then I might also be a gay.)

(Well obviously that's not true then, that's not true at all.)

(I am definitely, definitely not a gay.)

(I definitely like men.)

(But so does she. So did she. She had that boyfriend, Dave, that she went out with for ages. She had that other boyfriend, Stuart. She had that one called Andrew and that weird English boyfriend, Miles or Giles who lived on Mull, and that boy Sammy, and there was one called Tony, and Nicholas, because she always had boyfriends, she had boyfriends from about the age of twelve, long before I did.)

I am crossing at the lights. I am going to run as far as I can. I am going to run along the river, through the Islands, round by the sports tracks, past the cemetery and up towards the canal

(is that the right way to say it, a gay? Is there a correct word for it?)

(How do you know if you are it?)

(Does our mother know about Anthea being it?)

(Does our father know?)

(It is completely natural to be a gay or a homosexual or whatever. It is totally okay in this day and age.)

(Gay people are just the same as heterosexual people, except for the being gay, of course.)

(They were holding hands at the front door.)

(I should have known. She always was weird. She always was different. She always was contrary. She always did what she knew she shouldn't.)

(It is the fault of the Spice Girls.)

(She chose the video of Spiceworld with Sporty Spice on the limited edition tin.)

(She was always a bit too feminist.)

(She was always playing that George Michael cd.)

(She always votes for the girls on Big Brother and she voted for that transsexual the year he was on, or she, or whatever it is you're supposed to say.)

(She liked the Eurovision Song Contest.)

(She still likes the Eurovision Song Contest.)

(She liked Buffy the Vampire Slayer.)

(But so did I. I liked it too. And it had those girls in it who were both female homosexuals and they were portrayed as very sweet, and it was okay because it was Willow, and she was clever, and we knew to like her and everything, and her friend Tara was very sweet, and I remember one episode where they kissed and their feet came off the ground and they levitated because of the kiss, and I remember that the thing to do when we talked about it at school the next day was to make sick noises.)

Four texts on my phone. Dominic.

WOT U UP 2?

COMIN 2 PUB?

GET HERE NOW.

U R REQD HERE.

(I hate text language. It is so demeaning.)

(I will text him when I get back from my run. I will say I left my mobile at home and didn't get the message till later.)

I am down to just over seven stone.

I am doing well.

We are really revolutionising the bottled water market in Scotland.

Eau Caledonia. They love it as a tag. I got a raise.

I get paid thirty-five thousand before tax.

I can't believe I'm earning that much money. Me!

I am clearly doing the right thing. There is good money in water.

(She is still insisting on calling them shaveys or whatever, and it is unfair of her to lump them all together. It is just fashion. Boys are worse followers of fashion than girls. I mean, men than women. She is wrong to do that. She is wrong)

(they were holding hands at the front door, where any neighbour could see, and then I saw Robin Goodman lean my sister gently into the hedge, back against the branches of it, she was so gentle, and   )

(and kiss her.)

(I should have known when she always liked songs that had I and you in them, instead of he and I, or he and she, we always knew, we used to say at college that that was the giveaway, when people preferred those songs that had the word you instead of a man or a woman, like that classic old Tracy Chapman album our mother left behind her that she was always playing before she went.)

(I will never leave my children when I have fallen in love and am married and have had them. I will have them young, not when I am old, like the selfish generation. I would rather give up any career than not have them. I would rather give myself up. I would rather give up everything including any stupid political principle than leave children that belonged to me. Look how it ends. Thank God that feministy time of selfishness is over and we now have everything we will ever need, including a much more responsible set of values.)

It is a lovely day to go for a run. It is not raining. It doesn't even look like it will rain later.

(My sister is a gay.)

(I am not upset.) (I am fine.)

(It'd be okay, I mean I wouldn't mind so much, if it was someone else's sister.)

(It is okay. Lots of people are it. Just none that I have known personally, that's all.)

I am running along the riverside. I am so lucky to live here at this time in history, in the Capital of the Highlands, which is exceptionally buoyant right now, the fastest-developing city in the whole of the UK at the moment thanks to tourism and retirement, and soon also thanks to the growing water economy, of which I am a central part, and which will make history.

We speak the purest English here in the whole country. It is because of the vowel sounds and what happened to them when Gaelic speakers were made to speak English after the 1745 rebellion and the 1746 defeat when Gaelic was stamped out and punishable by death, and then all the local girls married the incoming English-speaking soldiers.

If I can remember the exact, correct words to all the songs on that awful Tracy Chapman album, which I can't have heard for years, it must be at least ten years, I'll be able to run for at least three more miles.

It is good to be goal-orientated. It makes all the other things go out of your mind.

I could go via the canal and past the locks and up over towards the Beauly road and then round by

(but dear God my sister has been hanging around for weeks with a person who is a criminal and against whom the company I work for is pressing charges, and not just that but a person whom I remember from school, and a person, I also remember, we all always called   that word   behind her back at school, and now this person has turned my sister into one of them, I mean One of Them. And I mean, how did we know to call Robin Goodman   that word   at school? Adolescent instinct? Well, I didn't know, I never really knew. I thought it was because she had a boy's name instead of a girl's name. That's what I used to think, or maybe because she came in on the bus from Beauly, with the Beauly kids, from somewhere else, and because she had a boy's name, that's what I thought. And because she was a bit different, and didn't people used to say that her mother was black, Robin Goodman, and her father was white, or was it the other way round, and was that even true? I don't remember there being any black people living in Beauly, we'd surely have known, we'd all have known, if there was.)

(I can't bring myself to say the word.)

(Dear God. It is worse than the word cancer.)

(My little sister is going to grow up into a dissatisfied older predatory totally dried-up abnormal woman like Judi Dench in that film Notes on a Scandal.)

(Judi Dench plays that sort of person so well, is what I thought when I saw it, but that was when I didn't think my sister was going to maybe be one of them and have such a terrible life with no real love in it.)

(My little sister is going to have a terrible sad life.)

(But I saw Robin Goodman lean my sister into the hedge with such gentleness, there is no other word for it, and kiss her, and then I saw, not so gently, Robin Goodman shift one of her own legs in between my sister's legs while she kissed her, and I saw my sister, it wasn't just one-sided, she was kissing Robin Goodman back, and then they were both laughing.)

(They were laughing with outrageous happiness.)

(Neighbours must have seen. It was broad daylight.)

(I might have to move house.)

(Well, that's all right. That's all right. If I have to move house I have enough money to.)

Thirty-five thousand, very good money for my age, and for me being a girl, our dad says, which is a bit sexist of him, because gender is nothing to do with whether you are good at a job or not. It is nothing to do with me being a woman or not, the fact that I am the only woman on the Highland Pure Creative board of ten of us — it is because I am good at what I do.

Actually, I think Keith might ask me to go to the States, maybe for training with the in-house Creatives at Base Camp. I think Base Camp is in LA!

He seems very pleased with the Eau Caledonia tag.

He thinks it will corner not just the English-speaking market but a good chunk of the French market, which is crucial, the French market being so water-sales-established

worldwide. Scottish, yet French. Well done, he said.
They'd like you at Base Camp. You'd like it there.

Me! Los Angeles!

He seemed to be intimating it. He intimated it last
Tuesday. He said I'd like it there, that's what he said
last week, that I'd like it, that they'd like me.

I told Anthea he had intimated it. She said: Keith
intubated you? Like on ER?

I said: you're being ridiculous, Anthea.

(There is also that gay woman doctor character on
ER whose lovers always die in fires and so on.)

(Gay people are always dying all the time.)

Anthea is being ridiculous. I got her a good position
and now she is at home doing nothing. She is really
clever. She is wasting herself.

(I was sitting at home trying to think of a tag, I'd
thought of MacAqua, but McDonald's would sue, I'd
thought of Scotteau, I'd been saying the word Eau out
loud, and Anthea walked past the table as I said it, and
she added Caledonia, we're such a good team, we'd be a
good team, we'd have been a good team, oh my God my
sister is a)

Well, it is bloody lucky Keith intimates anything to

me at all after they did me that favour at Pure about Anthea. She is so naïve, she has no idea what an unusually good salary level she was started at, it is really lucky nobody has associated me with how rude she was that day and that thing happening to the Pure sign

(which is clearly where they met. Maybe I saw the oh so romantic moment they met, last month, I was watching out the window, and the weirdo vandal came down the ladder and she and Anthea were talking, before Security took her away to wait for the police. I saw the name on the forms Security made her fill out. I recognised it. I knew it, the name, from when we were girls. It's a small town. What else can you do, in a small town?)

(Unless they were in cahoots before that and had decided on it as a dual attack on Pure, which is possible, I mean, anything under the sun is possible now.)

(Everything has changed.)

(Nothing is the same.)

I've stopped. I'm not running. I'm just standing.

(I don't want to run anywhere. I can't think where to run to.)

(I better make it look like there is a reason for me to

be just standing. I'll go and stand by the pedestrian crossing.)

That word *intimated* is maybe something to do with the word intimate, since the word intimate is so much a part of, almost the whole of, the word intimated.

I am standing at the pedestrian crossing like a (normal) person waiting to cross the road. A bus goes past. It is full of (normal-looking) people.

(My sister is now one of the reasons the man who owns Stagecoach buses had that million-pound poster campaign all over Scotland where they had pictures of people saying things like 'I'm not a bigot but I don't want my children taught to be gay at school', that kind of thing.)

(They were laughing. Like they were actually happy. Or like being gay is okay, or really funny, or really good fun, or something.)

I am running on the spot so as not to lose momentum.

(It is the putting of that leg in between the other legs that I can't get out of my head. It is really kind of unforgettable.)

(It is so . . .

intimate.)

I stop running on the spot. I stand at the pedestrian crossing and look one way, then the other. Nothing is coming. The road is totally clear.

But I just stand.

(I don't know what's the matter with me. I can't get myself to cross from one side to the other.)

(My sister would be banned in schools if she was a book.)

(No, because the parliament lifted that legislation, didn't it?)

(Did it?)

(I can't remember. I can't remember either way. I didn't ever think that particular law was anything I'd ever have to remember, or consider.)

(Have I ever noticed or considered anything about it? Should I have?)

(I did. I have. I remember reading in the paper about how people all across the world, and not just people but governments, in Poland and in Russia, but also in Spain, and Italy, are getting more and more tough on people being it. I mean, you'd expect that in Russia and in Poland. But in Italy? In Spain? Those are places that are supposed to be like here.)

(It said in the paper this morning that teenagers who are it are six times more likely to commit suicide than teenagers who aren't it.)

(I don't know what to do with myself.)

I stand at the crossing with no cars coming in either direction and I still don't move to cross the road. I feel a little dizzy. I feel a little faint.

(Anyone looking at me will think I'm really weird.)

There's only Dominic and Norman in the pub.

Where've you been, you useless slag? Norman says.

Don't call me that, I say.

Can't take a joke? he says. Loosen up. Ha ha!

He goes to the bar and brings me a glass of white.

Norm, I said a Diet Coke, I say.

But I've bought it now, Norman says.

So I see, I say.

Do you want me to take it back and change it? Norman says.

No, it's okay, I'll drink it since it's here now, I say.

I texted you, Madge, Dominic says.

(My name's Imogen.)

Did you? I say.

I texted you four times, Dominic says.

Ah. Because I left my mobile at home, I say.

I can't believe you didn't have your mobile with you, when I'd told you I was going to text you, Dominic says.

He looks really offended.

No Paul or anybody? I say. I thought everybody was coming.

Just us, Norman says. Your lucky night. Bri's coming later. He's bringing Chantelle.

I'd bring Chantelle any day, Dominic says.

I'd do a lot more to Chantelle than just bring her, Norman says. Paul's gay, man. He won't come out on a Monday night because of University Challenge being on.

Paul isn't gay, I say in a small voice.

Paul's hoping there'll be questions on tonight about Uranus, Dominic says.

Paul isn't gay, I say again louder.

You talking from experience then? Norman says.

Scintillating conversation, I say.

I make my face look bored. I hope it will work.

Dominic doesn't say anything. He just stares at me. The way he's looking at me makes me look away. I pretend I'm going to the ladies. I slip into the other bar and phone Paul.

Come to the pub, I say. I try to sound bright.

Who's there? Paul asks.

Loads of us, I say.

Is it Dom and Norm? Paul says. I'm only asking because they left an abusive message on my answerphone.

Uh huh. And me, I say. I'm here.

No offence, Imogen. But I'm not coming out, Paul says. They're wankers. They think they're so funny, they act like some nasty double act off tv. I don't know what you're doing out with them.

Go on, Paul, please, I say. It'll be good fun.

Yeah, but the world now divides into people who think it's good fun looking up pictures on the net of women fucking horses and dogs, and people who don't, Paul says. If you need me to come and get you, call me later.

Paul is very uptight, I think when I press the button to hang up.

I don't see why he can't just pretend to find it funny like the rest of us have to.

(Maybe he *is* gay.)

So what about that other work experience girl, then?
Norman is saying when I get back through. The one
who's not Chantelle. What about work-experiencing her?

I've other things in mind, Dominic says looking at
me.

I look above his eyes, at his forehead. I can't help
noticing that both Dominic and Norman have the exact
same haircut. Norman goes to the bar and comes back
with a full wine bottle. He and Dominic are drinking
Grolsch.

I can't drink all that, I say. I'm only out for one or
two, I've got to get back.

Yes you can, Norman says. He fills the glass up past
the little line, right to the very top, so that it's almost
spilling over onto the table, so that to drink anything
out of it at all I'm going to have to lean over and put
my mouth to it there on the table, or pick it up with
superhuman care so as not to spill it.

We're off for a curry in a minute, Dominic says.
You're coming too. Drink it fast.

I can't, I say. It's Monday. There's work tomorrow.

Yes you can, Norman says. We work too, you know.

I drink four glasses filled to the top like this. It

makes them roar with laughter when I bend right down to drink it. Eventually I do it so that that's what it will do, make them laugh.

At the restaurant, where everything smells too strong, and where the walls seem to be coming away from their skirting boards, they talk about work as if I'm not there. They make several jokes about Muslim pilots. They tell a long complicated joke about a blind Jewish man and a prostitute. Then Brian texts Dominic to say he can't come. This causes a shouted dialogue with him down the phone about Chantelle, about Chantelle's greggy friend, and about whether Chantelle's greggy friend is there with Chantelle right now so that Brian can 'watch'. Meanwhile I sit in the swirling restaurant and wonder what the word greggy means. It's clearly a word they've made up. It makes them really laugh. It makes them laugh so much that people round us are looking offended, and so are the Indian people serving us. I can't help laughing too.

The word seems to mean, on the whole, that they don't think the other work experience girl wears enough make-up to work, regardless of the fact she's sixteen and should really know how to by now, as Norman says.

That she wears the wrong kinds of clothes. That she is a bit of a disappointment.

That she's a bit, you know, greg, Dominic says.

I think I'm beginning to understand, I say.

I mean, take you. You exercise, and everything. You've got a top job, and everything. But that doesn't make you a greg. That bike you've got. You can get away with it, Norman says.

So the fact that I look all right on a motorbike means I'm not a greg? I say.

They both burst out laughing.

So it means unfeminine? I say.

I'd like to see her gregging, Norman says looking at me. You and that good-looking little sister of yours.

They roar with laughter. I am beginning to find the laughter a bit like someone is sandpapering my skull. I look away from the people all looking at us. I look down at the tablecloth.

Aw. She doesn't like not knowing the politically correct terms for things, Dominic says.

Greggy greggy greggy. Use your head, Norman says. Come on. Free associate.

Dreggy? I say. Something to do with dregs?

Getting there, getting there, Norman says.

Go on, give her a clue, Dominic says.

Okay. Here's a great big clue. Like the man at the BBC, Norman says.

What man? I say.

The man who got the sack for Iraq, who used to run the BBC until he let people say what they shouldn't have, out loud, on the news, Norman says.

Um, I say.

Are you retarded? Greg Dyke. Remember? Dominic says.

You mean, the work experience girl is something to do with Greg Dyke? I say.

They both laugh.

You mean, she says things out loud that she shouldn't? I say.

She's, like, a thespian, Norman says.

A what? I say.

A lickian, Norman says. Well, she looks like one.

Like that freakshow who daubed the Pure sign that day, Dominic says. Fucking dyke.

(My whole body goes cold.)

Now there's one trial I can't wait to see come to

court. I hope we all get to come to it, Norman is saying.

We will, Dominic says. They'll need men for there to be any coming at a trial like that.

Just what I was telling Brian, Norman says. Be ready to step in, now, when the moment's right.

You know, I say, it said in the paper this morning that teenagers who are gay are six times more likely to kill themselves than teenagers who aren't.

Good. Ha ha! Norman says.

Dominic's eyes cloud. Human species, self-patrolling, he says.

They start talking as if I'm not there again, like they did when they were talking about work.

See, that's what I don't get, Dominic says shaking his head, serious. Because, there's no way they could do it, I mean, without one. So it's like, pointless.

Freud defined it, Norman says (Norman did psychology at Stirling), as a state of lack. A state of lacking something really, you know, fundamental.

Dominic nods, grave-faced.

Exactly, he says. Obviously.

Adolescent backwardness. Marked underdevelopment, Norman says.

Yeah, but a really heavy case of underdevelopment, Dominic says. I mean, never mind anything else. Never mind how weird it is. Like, what gets me is, there's nothing to do the job. Nothing to do the jiggery-pokery with. And that's why Queen Victoria didn't make rugmunch illegal.

How's that? Norman says.

It was on Channel Four. Apparently she said there was no such thing, like, it didn't exist. And she was right. I mean, when men do it, poofs, in sexual terms, I mean, it's fucking disgusting and it leads to queer paedophilia and everything, but at least it's real sex they have, eh? But women. It's, like, how can they? I just don't get it. It's a joke, Dominic says.

Yeah, but it's good, Norman says, if you're watching and they're both fuckable.

Yeah, but the real ones are really mostly pretty unfuckable, you have to admit, Dominic says.

(Oh my God my sister who is related to me is a greg, a lack, unfuckable, not properly developed, and not even worth making illegal.)

(There are so many words I don't know for what my little sister is.)

Dominic and Norman are somehow roaring with laughter again. They have their arms round each other.

I have to go now, I say.

No you don't, they say in unison and fill my glass with Cobra.

Yes, I do, I say.

I shake them off at the multi-storey. I dodge behind a car so they don't know where I've gone. I wait there until the legs I can see moving about have disappeared. I hear them go up the stairs and I watch them fumble at the exit ticket machine until finally whichever one of them is driving finds the ticket, works out how to put it into the machine the right way and their car goes under the lifted barrier.

I throw up under a tree at the side of the road on my way home. I look up. The tree I've just been sick under is in full white blossom.

(Adolescent backwardness.)

(I am fourteen. Myself and Denise MacCall are in a geography classroom. It is interval. We have somehow managed to stay in; maybe Denise said she was feeling sick or maybe I did; that was how you got to stay in

over interval. We often said we felt sick if it was raining or cold.

There is a pile of homework jotters on the table.
Denise is going through them, reading out people's
names. We say out loud at each name whether we pass
or fail the person, like the game Anthea and I play at
home at the countdown of the chart on Top of the Pops.
Hurray for someone we like. Boo for someone we don't.

Denise finds Robin Goodman's jotter.

For some reason Denise MacCall really dislikes Robin
Goodman from Beauly, with her short curly dark hair
thick on top of her head, her darkish skin, her long
hands that the music teacher is always going on about
when she plays her clarinet, her serious, studious, far-
too-clever face. I dislike her too, though I hardly know
her. She is in two or three of my classes, that's all I
know about her, apart from that she plays the clarinet.
But it makes me feel happy to dislike her right now,
because this is proof that I am Denise's friend. Though I
am not so sure that I like Denise all that much either, or
that Denise wouldn't boo me if she got to a jotter with
my name on it and I wasn't here in the room with her.

Denise and I write the letters L, E and Z, on the

front of Robin Goodman's jotter, with the black Pentel I
have in my pencil case. Or, to be more exact, I write
the letters and she draws the arrow pointing at them.

Then we slide the jotter back into the middle of the
pile.

When geography class starts, and Horny Geog,
which is what we call Miss Horne, the old lady
teacher who teaches us it, gives out the jotters, we
watch to see Robin Goodman's response. I am sitting a
couple of rows behind her. I see her shoulders tense,
then droop.

When I go past her at the end of the period and
glance down at the book on her desk I can see that
she's made Denise's arrow into the trunk of a tree and
she's drawn hundreds of little flowerheads, all around
the letters L, E and Z, like the letters are the branches
of the tree and they've all just come into bloom.)

The same Robin Goodman, ten years later, with her
long dark hair and her dark, serious, studious face, is
(oh my God)
right here in my house when I get home. She is
sitting on the couch with a cup of tea in front of her.

She is reading a book. I am too drunk and dizzy to make out the cover of the book she is reading. I stand in the doorway and hold on to the doorframe.

Hi, she says.

(Oh my God and also my sister is a)

What have you done with my sister? I say.

Your sister's in the bath, she says.

I sit down. I lean my head back. I feel sick.

(I am sitting in the same room as a)

Robin Goodman leaves the room. When she comes back, she puts something into my hand. It's a glass. It's one of my glasses from the cupboard.

Drink that, she says, and I'll get you another one.

You haven't changed much, since school, I say. You look exactly the same.

So do you, she says. But some things have changed, thank God. We're not schoolgirls any more.

Apart from. Your hair. Got longer, I say.

Well, ten years, she says. Something's got to give.

I went away to unversity, I say. Did you go?

If you mean university, yes, I did, she says.

And you came back, I say.

Just like you, she says.

Do you still play the clarnet? I say.

No, she says.

There's a silence. I look down. There's a glass in my
hand.

Drink it, she says.

I drink it. It tastes beautiful, of clearness.

That'll be better, she says.

She takes the empty glass and leaves the room. I hear
her in my kitchen. I look down at myself and am
surprised to see I'm still wearing the tracksuit I put on
after work. I'm not completely sure where I've just
been. I begin to wonder if I made up the whole evening,
if I invented the pub, the curryhouse, the whole thing.

That's my kitchen you were just in, I say when she
comes back through.

I know, she says and sits down in my sitting room.

This is my sitting room, I say.

Yep, she says.

(I am sitting in the same room as a)

She is the kind of person who does not really care
what she is wearing or what it looks like. At least she is
wearing normal clothes. At least she is not wearing that
embarrassing Scottish get-up.

Not wearing your kilt tonight? I say.

Only for special occasions, she says.

My company that I work for, you know, Pure Incorported, is going to take you to court, I say.

They'll drop the charges, she says.

She doesn't even look up from her book. I have to look at my hand because it's covered in the water I've spilled on myself. I hold the glass up and look through it. I look at the room through the bit with water in it. Then I look at the same room through the bit with no water in it. Then I drink the water.

Eau Caledonia, I say.

Need another? she says.

(I am sitting in the same room as a)

A lass and a lack, I say.

This pun makes me laugh. It is unlike me to be witty. It is my sister who is the really witty one. I am the one who knows the correct words, the right words for things.

I lean forward.

Tell me what it is, I say.

It's water, Robin Goodman says.

No, I say. I mean, what's the correct word for it, I

mean, for you? I need to know it. I need to know the proper word.

She looks at me for a long time. I can feel her looking right through my drunkness. Then, when she speaks, it is as if the whole look of her speaks.

The proper word for me, Robin Goodman says, is me.

us

Because of us, things came together. Everything was possible.

I had not known, before us, that every vein in my body was capable of carrying light, like a river seen from a train makes a channel of sky etch itself deep into a landscape. I had not really known I could be so much more than myself. I had not known another body could do this to mine.

Now I'd become a walking fuse, like in that poem about the flower, and the force, and the green fuse the force drives through it; the force that blasts the roots of trees was blasting the roots of me, I was like a species that hadn't even realised it lived in a near-desert till one day its taproot hit water. Now I had taken a whole new shape. No, I had taken the shape I was always supposed to, the shape that let me hold my head high. Me, Anthea Gunn, head turned towards the sun.

Your name, Robin had said on our first underwater

night together deep in each other's arms. It means flowers, did you know that?

No it doesn't, I'd said. Gunn means war. The clan motto is Either Peace or War. Midge and I did a clan project at school when I was small.

No, I mean your first name, she said.

I was named after someone off the tv, I said.

It means flowers, or a coming-up of flowers, a blooming of flowers, she said. I looked you up.

She was behind me in the bed, she was speaking into my shoulder.

You, she was saying. You're a walking peace protest. You're the flower in the Gunn.

And what about you? I said. I tried looking you up too. I did it before we'd even met. What does the weird name mean?

What weird name? she said.

It isn't in the dictionary, I said. I looked. I Googled you. It doesn't mean anything.

Everything means something, she said.

Iphisol, I said.

Iff is sol? she said. Iffisol? I don't know. I've no idea. It sounds like aerosol. Or Anusol.

She was holding me loosely, her arms were round me and one leg over my legs keeping me warm, I could feel the smooth new skin of her from my shoulders down to my calves. Then the bed was shaking; she was laughing.

Not Iffisol. Eye fizz ol, she said. Iphis is said like eye fizz. And it's not ol, it's 07. Like, the name, Iphis, but with the year, the oh and the seven of two thousand and seven.

Oh. Iphis oh seven. Oh, I said.

I was laughing now too. I turned in her arms and put my head on her laughing collarbone.

Like double oh seven. Daniel Craig in Casino Royal, rising out of the water like that goddess on a shell, I said. Lo and behold.

Ursula Andress did it first, she said. I mean, after Venus herself, that is. In fact, Daniel Craig and Ursula Andress look remarkably alike, when you compare them. No, because last year I used Iphis06. The year before I was Iphis05. God knows what you'd have thought *they* said. Iffisog. Iffisos.

It had been exciting, first the not knowing what Robin was, then the finding out. The grey area, I'd discovered, had been misnamed: really the grey area was a whole other spectrum of colours new to the eye. She had the swagger of a girl. She blushed like a boy. She had a girl's toughness. She had a boy's gentleness. She was as meaty as a girl. She was as graceful as a boy. She was as brave and handsome and rough as a girl. She was as pretty and delicate and dainty as a boy. She turned boys' heads like a girl. She turned girls' heads like a boy. She made love like a boy. She made love like a girl. She was so boyish it was girlish, so girlish it was boyish, she made me want to rove the world writing our names on every tree. I had simply never found anyone so right. Sometimes this shocked me so much that I was unable to speak. Sometimes when I looked at her, I had to look away. Already she was like no one else to me. Already I was fearful she would go. I was used to people being snatched away. I was used to the changes that came out of the blue. The old blue, that is. The blue that belonged to the old spectrum.

My grandfather used to say that all the time, lo and behold, I told her. They're dead, my grandparents. They drowned. This used to be their house.

Tell me about them, she said.

You tell me about you first, I said. Come on. Story of your life.

I will, she said. Yours first.

If my life was a story, I said, it'd start like this: Before she left, my mother gave me a compass. But when I tried to use it, when I was really far out, lost at sea, the compass didn't work. So I tried the other compass, the one my father had given me before he left. But that compass was broken too.

So you looked out across the deep waters, Robin said. And you decided, by yourself, and with the help of a clear night and some stars, which way was north and which was south and which way was east and which was west. Yes?

Yes, I said.

Then I said it again. Yes.

Now do you want to know mine? she said.

I do, I said.

It begins one day when I come down a ladder off an interventionist act of art protest, and turn round and see the most beautiful person I've ever seen. From that moment on, I'm home. It's as if I've been struggling upstream, going against the grain, until that moment.

Then we get married, me and the person, and we live together happily ever after, which is impossible, both in story and in life, actually. But we get to. And that's the message. That's it. That's all.

What sort of story's that? I said.

A very fishy sort, she said.

It sounds a bit lightweight, as stories go, I said.

I can be heavy-handed if you want, she said. Fancy a bit of heavy-handing? Or would you prefer something lighter? You choose.

Then she held me tight.

Lo and be held, she said.

You're very artful, you, I said.

You're not so bad yourself, she said.

We woke up. It was light. It was half past two in the morning. We got up and opened the window; we leaned together on the sill and watched the world wake up, and as the birds fought to be heard above one another before all the usual noise of day set in to drown them out she told me the story of Iphis.

A long time ago on the island of Crete a woman was pregnant and when the time came close to her giving birth her husband, a good man, came to her and said, if it's a boy we'll keep him, but if it's a girl we can't. We can't afford a girl, she'll have to be put to death, I'm so sorry, but it's just the way things are. So the woman went to the temple and prayed to the goddess Isis, who miraculously appeared before her. You've been true to me so I'll be true to you, the goddess said. Bring the child up regardless of what it is and I promise you everything will be fine. So the child was born and it was a girl. The mother brought her up secretly as a boy, calling her Iphis, which was a name both boys and girls could be called. And Iphis went to school and was educated with her friend Ianthe, the beautiful daughter of a fine family, and Iphis and Ianthe grew up looking into each other's eyes. Love touched their innocent hearts simultaneously and wounded them both, and they were betrothed. As the wedding day approached and the whole of Crete prepared for the celebration, Iphis got more and more worried about how, being a girl like Ianthe, she would ever be able to please her bride, whom she so loved. She worried that she herself would never really enjoy her bride the way she longed to. She complained bitterly to the gods and goddesses

about it. On the night before the wedding, Iphis's
mother went back to the temple and asked the goddess
to help. As she left the empty temple its walls shook,
its doors trembled, Iphis's jaw lengthened, her stride
lengthened, her ribcage widened and broadened, her
chest flattened, and the next day, the wedding day,
dawned bright and clear and there was rejoicing all over
the island of Crete as the boy Iphis gained his own
Ianthe.

Though actually, the telling of it went much more like
this:

A long time ago, on the island of Crete, Robin said
behind me, into my ear —

I've been there! We went there! I said. We had a holiday there when we were kids. We spent a lot of it at
the hospital in Heraklion, actually, because our dad
went to hire a motorbike to impress this woman in a
motorbike hire shop, and before he'd hired one he rode
it a few yards round a corner to get a feel for it, and
fell off it and scraped the skin off half the side of his
body.

A long time ago, Robin said, long before motorbike

hire, long before motors, long before bikes, long before
you, long before me, back before the great tsunami that
flattened most of northern Crete and drowned most of
the Minoan cities, which, by the way, was probably the
incident responsible for the creation of the myth about
the lost city of Atlantis –

That's very interesting, I said.

It is, she said. There's pumice stone fifty feet up on
dry land in parts of Crete, and cow-bones all mixed up
with sea-creature remains, far too high for any other
geological explanation –

No, I mean that thing about responsibility and creat-
ing a myth, I said.

Oh, she said. Well –

I mean, do myths spring fully formed from the
imagination and the needs of a society, I said, as if they
emerged from society's subconscious? Or are myths
conscious creations by the various money-making forces?
For instance, is advertising a new kind of myth-making?
Do companies sell their water etc by telling us the right
kind of persuasive myth? Is that why people who really
don't need to buy something that's practically free still
go out and buy bottles of it? Will they soon be thinking

up a myth to sell us air? And do people, for instance, want to be thin because of a prevailing myth that thinness is more beautiful?

Anth, Robin said. Do you want to hear this story about the boy-girl or don't you?

I do, I said.

Right. Crete. Way back then, she said. Ready?

Uh huh, I said.

Sure? she said.

Yep, I said.

So there was this woman who was pregnant, and her husband came to her —

Which one was Iphis? I said.

Neither, she said. And her husband said —

What were their names? I said.

I can't remember their names. Anyway, the husband came to the wife —

Who was pregnant, I said.

Uh huh, and he said, listen, I'm really praying for two things, and one of them is that this baby gives you no pain in the giving birth.

Hmm, right, his wife said. That's likely, isn't it?

Ha ha! I said.

No, well, no she didn't, Robin said. I'm imposing far too modern a reading on it. No, she acted correctly for her time, thanked him for even considering, so graciously, from his man's world where women didn't really count, that there'd be any pain at all involved for her. And what's the other thing you're praying for? she asked. When she said this, the man, who was a good man, looked very sad. The woman was immediately suspicious. Her husband said, look, you know what I'm going to say. The thing is. When you give birth, if you have a boy, that'll be fine, we can keep it, of course, and that's what I'm praying for.

Uh huh? the woman said. And?

And if you have a girl, we can't, he said. We'll have to put it to death if it's a girl. A girl's a burden. You know it is. I can't afford a girl. You know I can't. A girl's no use to me. So that's that. I'm so sorry to have to say this, I wish it wasn't so, and I don't want to do this, but it's the way of the world.

The way of the world, I said. Great. Thank God we're modern.

Still the way of the world in lots of places all over

the world, Robin said, red ink for a girl, blue for a boy, on the bottom of doctors' certificates, letting parents know, in the places it's not legal to allow people just to abort girls, what to abort and what to keep. So. The woman went off to do some praying of her own. And as she knelt down in the temple, and prayed to the nothing that was there, the goddess Isis appeared right in front of her.

Like the Virgin Mary at Lourdes, I said.

Except much, much earlier, culturally and historically, than the Virgin Mary, Robin said, and also the woman wasn't sick, though certainly there was something pretty rotten in the state of Knossos, what with the whole kill-the-girl thing. And the goddess Isis had brought a lot of her god-friends and family with her, including that god whose head is like a jackal. What's his name? Damn. I really like – he's got, like, these jackal ears, and a long snout – a kind of dog-god – he guards the underworld –

I don't know. Is it a crucial part of the story? I said.

No. So Isis thanked the woman for the constant faith she had in things, and told her not to worry. Just give birth as per usual, and bring the child up, she said.

As per usual? I said. A goddess used the phrase *as per usual*?

The gods can be down-to-earth when they want, Robin said. And then she and all her god-friends disappeared, like they'd never been there, like the woman had just made them up. But the woman was very happy. She went and stood under the night sky and held her arms out open to the stars. And the time came for the baby to be born. And out it came.

You can't stay in the womb all your life, I said.

And it was a girl, Robin said.

Of course, I said.

So the woman called her Iphis, which was the child's grandfather's name –

I like that, I said.

– and was also, by chance, a name used both for girls and boys, which the woman thought was a good omen.

I like that too, I said.

And to keep her child safe she brought her up as a boy, Robin said. Lucky for Iphis, she looked rather good as a boy, though she'd also have looked very handsome as a girl. She was certainly every bit as handsome as her friend, Ianthe, the beautiful fair-haired daughter of one of the finest families on the island.

Aha, I said. I think I see where this is going.

And Iphis and Ianthe, since they were exactly the same age, went to school together, learned to read together, learned about the world together, grew up together, and as soon as they were both of marrying age their fathers did some bargaining, swapped some livestock, and the village got ready for the wedding. But not just that. The thing is, Iphis and Ianthe had actually, for real, very really, fallen in love.

Did their hearts hurt? I said. Did they think they were underwater all the time? Did they feel scoured by light? Did they wander about not knowing what to do with themselves?

Yes, Robin said. All of that. And more.

There's more? I said. Man!

So to speak, Robin said. And the wedding day was set. And the whole village was coming. Not just the village, but all the fine families of the island were coming. And some people off faraway other islands. And off the mainland. Several gods had been invited and many had actually said they'd come. And Iphis was in quite a bad way, because she couldn't imagine.

She couldn't imagine what? I said.

She couldn't imagine how she was going to do it, Robin said.

How do you mean? I said.

She stood in a field far enough away from the village so nobody would hear except maybe a few goats, a few cows, and she shouted at the sky, she shouted at nothing, at Isis, at all the gods. Why have you done this to me? You fuckers. You jokers. Look what's happened now. I mean, look at that cow there. What'd be the point in giving her a cow instead of a bull? I can't be a boy to my girl! I don't know how! I wish I'd never been born! You've made me wrong! I wish I'd been killed at birth! Nothing can help me!

But maybe her girl, what's her name, Ianthe, *wants* a girl, I said. Clearly Iphis is exactly the kind of boy-girl or girl-boy she loves.

Well, yes. I agree, Robin said. That's debatable. But it's not in the original story. In the original, Iphis stands there shouting at the gods. Even if Daedalus was here, Iphis shouted, and he's the greatest inventor in the world, who can fly across the sea like a bird though he's just a man! But even *he* wouldn't know what to invent to make this okay for Ianthe and me. I mean, you were kind, Isis, and you told my mother it'd be fine, but now what? Now I've got to get married, and it's tomorrow, and I'll be the laughing stock of the whole village, because of you. And Juno and Hymen are coming. We'll be the laughing stock of the heavens too. And how can I get married to my girl in front of them, in front of my father, in front of everyone? And not just that. Not just that. I'm never, ever, ever going to be able to please my girl. And she'll be mine, but never really mine. It'll be like standing right in the middle of a stream, dying of thirst, with my hand full of water, but I won't be able to drink it!

Why won't she be able to drink it? I said.

Robin shrugged.

It's just what she thinks at this point in the story, she said. She's young. She's scared. She doesn't know yet that it'll be okay. She's only about twelve. That was the marriageable age, then, twelve. I was terrified, too, when I was twelve and wanted to marry another girl. (Who did you want to marry? I said. Janice McLean, Robin said, who lived in Kinmylies. She was very glamorous. And she had a pony.) Twelve, or thirteen, terrified. It's easy to think it's a mistake, or you're a mistake. It's easy, when everything and everyone you know tells you you're the wrong shape, to believe you're the wrong shape. And also, don't forget, the story of Iphis was being made up by a man. Well, I say man, but Ovid's very fluid, as writers go, much more than most. He knows, more than most, that the imagination doesn't have a gender. He's really good. He honours all sorts of love. He honours all sorts of story. But with this story, well, he can't help being the Roman he is, he can't help fixating on what it is that girls don't have under their togas, and it's him who can't imagine what girls would ever do without one.

I had a quick look under the duvet.

Doesn't feel or look like anything's missing to me, I said.

Ah, I love Iphis, Robin said. I love her. Look at her. Dressed as a boy to save her life. Standing in a field, shouting at the way things are. She'd do anything for love. She'd risk changing everything she is.

What's going to happen? I said.

What do you think? Robin said.

Well, she's going to need some help. The father's not going to be any good, he doesn't even know his boy's a girl. Not very observant. And Ianthe thinks that's what a boy is, what Iphis is. Ianthe's just happy to be getting married. But she won't want a humiliation either, and they'd be the joke of the village. She's only twelve, too. So Iphis can't go and ask her for help. So. It's either the mother or the goddess.

Well-spotted, Robin said. Off the mother went to have a word with the goddess in her own way.

That's one of the reasons Midge is so resentful, I said.

The what who's so what? Robin said.

Imogen. She had to do all that mother stuff when ours left, I said. Maybe it's why she's so thin. Have you noticed how thin she is?

Yep, Robin said.

I never had to do anything, I said. I'm lucky. I was born mythless. I grew up mythless.

No you didn't. Nobody grows up mythless, Robin said. It's what we do with the myths we grow up with that matters.

I thought about our mother. I thought about what she'd said, that she had to be free of what people

expected of her, otherwise she'd simply have died. I
thought about our father, out in the garden in the first
days after she went, hanging out the washing. I thought
about Midge, seven years old, running downstairs to
take over, to do it instead of him, because the neighbours were laughing to see a man at the washing line.
Good girl, our father had said.

Keep telling the story, I said. Go on.

So the mother, then, Robin said, went to the temple,
and she said into the thin air: look, come on. You told
me it'd be okay. And now we've got this huge wedding
happening tomorrow, and it's all going to go wrong. So
could you just sort it out for me? Please.

And as she left the empty temple, the temple started
to shake, and the doors of the temple trembled.

And lo and behold, I said.

Yep. Jaw lengthens, stride lengthens, absolutely
everything lengthens. By the time she'd got home, the
girl Iphis had become exactly the boy that she and her
girl needed her to be. And the boy their two families
needed. And everyone in the village needed. And all the
people coming from all over the place who were very
anxious to have a really good party needed. And the

visiting gods needed. And the particular historic era with its own views on what was excitingly perverse in a love story needed. And the writer of Metamorphoses needed, who really, really needed a happy love story at the end of Book 9 to carry him through the several much more scurrilous stories about people who fall, unhappily and with terrible consequences, in love with their fathers, their brothers, various unsuitable animals, and the dead ghosts of their lovers, Robin said. Voilà. Sorted. No problemo. Metamorphoses is full of the gods being mean to people, raping people then turning them into cows or streams so they won't tell, hunting them till they change into plants or rivers, punishing them for their pride or their arrogance or their skill by changing them into mountains or insects. Happy stories are rare in it. But the next day dawned, and the whole world opened its eyes, it was the day of the wedding. Even Juno had come, and Hymen was there too, and all the families of Crete were gathered in their finery for the huge celebration all over the island, as the girl met her boy there at the altar.

Girl meets boy, I said. In so many more ways than one.

Old, old story, Robin said.

I'm glad it worked out, I said.

Good old story, Robin said.

Good old Ovid, giving it balls, I said.

Even though it didn't need them. Anubis! Robin said suddenly. The god with the jackal head. Anubis.

Anubis colony? I said.

Come on, Robin said. You and me. What do you say?

Bed, I said.

Off we went, back to bed.

We were tangled in each other's arms so that I wasn't sure whose hand that was by my head, was it hers or mine? I moved my hand. The hand by my head didn't move. She saw me looking at it.

It's yours, she said. I mean, it's on the end of my arm. But it's yours. So's the arm. So's the shoulder. So's everything else it's connected to.

Her hand opened me. Then her hand became a wing. Then everything about me became a wing, a single wing, and she was the other wing, we were a bird. We were a bird that could sing Mozart. It was a music I recognised, it was both deep and light. Then it changed into a music I'd never heard before, so new to me that it made me airborne, I was nothing but the notes she was playing, held in air. Then I saw her smile so close to my eyes that there was nothing to see but the smile, and the thought came into my head that I'd never been inside a smile before, who'd have thought being inside a smile would be so ancient and so modern both at once? Her beautiful head was down at my breast, she caught me between her teeth just once, she put the nip into nipple like the cub of a fox would, down we went, no wonder they call it an earth, it was loamy, it was good, it was what good meant, it was earthy, it was what earth meant, it was the underground of everything, the kind of soil that cleans things. Was that her tongue? Was that what they meant when they said flames had tongues? Was I melting? Would I melt? Was I gold? Was I magnesium? Was I briny, were my whole insides a piece of sea, was I nothing but salty water with a mind of its own, was I some kind of fountain, was I the force of water through stone? I was hard all right, and then I was sinew, I was a snake, I changed stone to snake in three simple moves, stoke stake snake, then I was a tree whose branches were all budded knots, and what were

those felty buds, were they — antlers? were antlers
really growing out of both of us? was my whole front
furring over? and were we the same pelt? were our
hands black shining hoofs? were we kicking? were we
bitten? were our heads locked into each other to the
death? till we broke open? I was a she was a he was a we
were a girl and a girl and a boy and a boy, we were
blades, were a knife that could cut through myth, were
two knives thrown by a magician, were arrows fired by
a god, we hit heart, we hit home, we were the tail of a
fish were the reek of a cat were the beak of a bird were
the feather that mastered gravity were high above every
landscape then down deep in the purple haze of the
heather were roamin in a gloamin in a brash unending
Scottish piece of perfect jigging reeling reel can we
really keep this up? this fast? this high? this happy?
round again? another notch higher? heuch! the perfect
jigsaw fit of one into the curve of another as if a hill
top into sky, was that a thistle? was I nothing but grass,
a patch of coarse grasses? was that incredible colour
coming out of me? the shining heads of — what? butter-
cups? because the scent of them, farmy and delicate,
came into my head and out of my eyes, my ears, out of

my mouth, out of my nose, I was scent that could see, I was eyes that could taste, I loved butter. I loved everything. Hold everything under my chin! I was all my open senses held together on the head of a pin, and was it an angel who knew how to use hands like that, as wings?

We were all that, in the space of about ten minutes. Phew. A bird, a song, the insides of a mouth, a fox, an earth, all the elements, minerals, a water feature, a stone, a snake, a tree, some thistles, several flowers, arrows, both genders, a whole new gender, no gender at all and God knows how many other things including a couple of fighting stags.

I got up to get us a drink of water and as I stood in the kitchen in the early morning light, running the water out of the tap, I looked out at the hills at the back of the town, at the trees on the hills, at the bushes in the garden, at the birds, at the brand new leaves on a branch, at a cat on a fence, at the bits of wood that made the fence, and I wondered if everything I saw, if maybe every landscape we casually glanced at, was the outcome of an ecstasy we didn't even know was happening, a love-act moving at a speed slow and steady enough for us to be deceived into thinking it was just everyday reality.

Then I wondered why on earth would anyone ever stand in the world as if standing in the cornucopic middle of the Hanging Gardens of Babylon but inside a tiny white-painted rectangle about the size of a single space in a car park, refusing to come out of it, and all round her or him the whole world, beautiful, various, waiting?

them

(It is really English down here in England.)

First class all the way. I was the only person in Carriage J when we set off. Me! A whole train carriage to myself! I am doing all right

(and that train getting more and more English the further south we came. The serving staff doing the coffee changed into English people at Newcastle. And the conductor's voice on the speakers changed into English at Newcastle too and then it was like being on a totally different train though I hadn't even moved in my seat, and the people getting on and sitting in the other seats round me all really Englishy and by the time we'd got to York it was like a different)

OUCH. Oh sorry!

(People in England just walk into you and they don't even apologise.)

(And there are so many, so many! People here go on and on for miles and miles and miles.)

(Where's my phone?)

Menu. Contacts. Select. Dad. Call.

(God, it is so busy here with the people and the noise and the traffic I can hardly hear the)

Answerphone.

(He never answers it when he sees my name come up.)

Hi Dad, it's me. It's Thursday, it's a quarter to five. Just leaving you another to tell you I'm not in first class on the train any more, I'm in that, eh, Leicester Square, God it's really sunny down here, it's a bit too warm, I've got half an hour between very important business meetings so was just calling to say hi. Eh, right, well, I'll give you a wee call when I'm out of my meetings, so bye for now. Bye now. Bye.

End call.

Menu. Contacts. Select. Paul. Call.

Answerphone.

(Damn.)

Oh hi Paul, it's just me, it's just eh Imogen. It's Thursday, it's about a quarter to five, and I was just wondering if you could check with secretarial for me, I eh can't get through, I've been trying and it's constantly

engaged or maybe something's up with the signal or
something, anyway sorry to be calling so late in the
afternoon, but because I couldn't get through I thought
what'll I do, oh I know, I can always phone Paul, he'll
help me out, so if you'd just check with them for me
that the market projection email and the colour print-
outs went off to Keith down here and whether he'll
have seen it all before I get over to the office? I should
be there in about fifteen minutes. I'll wait for your call,
Paul. Thanks, Paul. Bye for now. Bye now. Bye.

Menu. Contacts. Select. Anthea. Call.

Answerphone.

*Hi. This is Anthea. Don't leave me a message on this phone
because I'm actually trying not to use my mobile any longer
since the production of mobiles involves slave labour on a huge
scale and also since mobiles get in the way of us living fully
and properly in the present moment and connecting properly, on
a real level, with people and are just another way to sell us
short. Come and see me instead and we'll talk properly. Thanks.*

(For God's sake.)

Hi, it's me. It's Thursday, it's ten to five. Can you
hear me? I can hardly hear myself, it's so noisy here, it's
just ridiculous. Anyway I'm on my way to a meeting

and I was walking through a kind of a park or square at
the back of the Leicester Square, where I got the underground to, and there was this statue of William
Shakespeare there in it, and the thought came into my
head, Anthea'd like that, and then, like, you wouldn't
believe it! About two seconds later I saw right across
from it this statue of Charlie Chaplin! So I thought I'd
just phone and tell you. I'm actually coming up to
Trafalgar Square now, it's all, like, pedestrian now, you
can walk right across it, the fountains are on, it's so
warm down here that people are actually jumping about
in the water, it can't be hygienic, loads of people are
wearing shorts down here, nobody's got a coat on, I've
actually had to take mine off, that's how warm it is, oh!
and there's Nelson! but he's like so high up you can't
really see him at all, I'm right under him now, anyway I
was just phoning, because every time I come here and
see the famous things it makes me think of us, you
know, watching tv, when we were kids, and Nelson's
Column and Big Ben and wondering if we'd ever in a
million years get to see them really, for real, eh, well
now I'm waiting for the green man at a pedestrian
crossing right under Nelson's Column, you should hear

all the different languages, all round me, it's very very interesting to hear so many different voices at once, oh well, now I'm on a road that's all official-looking buildings, well, just calling to say I'll see you when I get back, I'm back tomorrow, I'll have to have a wee look at my map now, I'll have to get it out of my bag, so, well, I'll stop now. Bye for now. Bye.

End call.

(Still no Paul.)

(She won't ever hear that message. That message'll just delete itself off Orange in a week's time.)

(But it was nice to be talking on my phone here, made me feel a bit safer, and though I was ostensibly just saying stuff for no reason it kind of felt good to.)

(Maybe it's easier to talk to someone who won't ever actually hear what you say.)

(What a funny thought. What a ridiculous thought.)

Is this Strand?

(She loves all that Shakespeare stuff, and she loved that film, so did I, where the posh people are unveiling the new white statue and they pull the cover off and lying fast asleep in its arms is Charlie Chaplin, and later the blind girl gets her sight back because he gets rich with a windfall and spends it all on her sight operation, but then he sees that now that she can see, he's clearly the wrong kind of person, and it's tragic, not a comedy at all.)

(Still no Paul.)

(I can't see a streetname. I think I might not be on the right road for)

(oh look at that, that's an interesting-looking one, right in the middle of the road, what is it, a memorial? It's a memorial with just, as if empty clothes are hanging all round it on hooks, like empty clothes, a lot of soldiers' and workers' clothes.)

(But they look strange. They look like they've got the shapes of bodies still in them. And though they're men's clothes, the way all their folds are falling looks like women's –)

(Oh, right, it's a statue to the women who fought in the war. Oh I get it. It's like the clothes they wore, which they just took off and hung up, like a minute ago, like someone else's clothes they just stepped into briefly. And the clothes have kept their shape so that you get the bodyshape of women but in dungarees and uniforms and clothes they wouldn't usually wear and so on.)

(London is all statues. Look at that one. Look at him up on his high horse. I wonder who he was. It says on the side. I can't make it out. I wonder if he actually looked like he looks there, when he was alive. The Chaplin one didn't look anything like Chaplin, not really. And the Shakespeare one, well, no way of knowing.)

(Still no Paul.)

(I wonder why they didn't get to be people, like him, with faces and bodies, those women, they just got to be gone, they just got to be empty clothes.)

(Was it because there were too many girls and it had to be symbolic of them all?)

(But no, because there are always faces on the soldiers on war memorials, I mean the soldiers on those memorials get to be actual people, with bodies, not just clothes.)

(I wonder if that's better, just clothes, I mean in terms of art and meaning and such like. Is it better, like more symbolic, *not* to be there?)

(Anthea would know.)

(I mean, what if Nelson was symbolised by just a hat and an empty jacket? Sometimes Chaplin is just a hat and boots and a walking stick or a hat and a moustache. But that's because he's so individual that you know who he is from those things.)

(Both our grandmothers were in that war. Those clothes on that memorial are the empty clothes of our grandmothers.)

(The faces of our grandmothers. We never even saw our mother's mother's face, well, only in photos we saw it. She was dead before we were born.)

(Still no Paul.)

That sign says Whitehall.

I'm on the wrong road.

(God, Imogen, can't you do anything right?)

I better go back.

My ambition, Keith says, is to make Pure oblivion possible.

Right! I say.

(I hope I say it brightly enough.)

What I want, he says, is to make it not just possible but natural for someone, from the point of rising in the morning to the point of going to sleep again at night, to spend his whole day, obliviously, in Pure hands.

So, when his wife turns on his tap to fill his coffee machine, the water that comes out of it is administered, tested and cleaned by Pure. When she puts his coffee in the filter and butters his toast, or chooses him an apple from the fruit bowl, each of these products will have been shipped by and bought at one of the outlets belonging to Pure. When he picks up the paper to read at the breakfast table, whether it's a tabloid or a Berliner or a broadsheet, it's one of the papers that belong to Pure. When he switches on his computer, the server he uses is Pure-owned, and the breakfast tv programme he's not really watching is going out on one of the channels the majority of whose shares is held by Pure. When his wife changes the baby's diaper, it's replaced with one bought and packed by Pure Pharmaceuticals, like the two ibuprofen she's just about to neck, and all the other drugs she needs to take in the course of the day, and when his baby eats, it eats bottled organic range Ooh Baby, made and distributed by Pure. When he slips the latest paperback into his briefcase, or when his wife thinks about what she'll be reading at her book group later that day, whatever it is has been published by one of the twelve imprints owned by Pure, and bought, in person or online, at one of the three chains now owned by Pure, and if it was bought online it may even have been delivered by a mail network operated by Pure. And should our man feel like watching some high-grade porn, – if you'll excuse me, ah, ah, for being so crude as to suggest it –

I nod.

(I smile like people suggest it to me all the time.)

– on his laptop or on his phonescreen on the way to work, while he keeps himself hydrated by drinking a bottle of Pure's Eau Caledonia, he can do so courtesy of one of the several leisure outlets owned, distributed and operated by Pure.

(But I am feeling a bit uneasy. I am feeling a bit disenchanted. Has Keith driven me all this way out of London in a specially-chauffeured car to this collection of prefab offices on the outskirts of a New Town just to give me a Creative lecture?)

And that's just breakfast, Keith is saying. Our Pure Man hasn't even reached work yet. That's just the opener. There's the whole rest of the day to come. And we've only touched on his wife, only skimmed the surface of his infant. We haven't even begun to consider his ten-year-old son, his teenage daughter. Because Pure Product is everywhere. Pure is massive throughout the global economy.

But most important, Pure is pure. And Pure must be perceived by the market as pure. It does what it says on the tin. You get me, ah, ah ?

Imogen, Keith, yes, Keith, I do, I say.

Keith is walking me from prefab to prefab, holding forth. There seems to be almost nobody else working here.

(Maybe they've all gone home. It's seven p.m., after all.)

(I wish there were at least one or two other people around. I wish that chauffeur bloke had stayed. But no, he pulled out of the car park as soon as he dropped me off.)

(The angle the sun is at is making it hard for me to do anything but squint at Keith.)

Right, Keith, I say

(even though he hasn't said anything else.)

(He isn't in the least bit interested in the print-outs. I've tried bringing them into the conversation twice.)

. . . trillion-dollar water market, he is saying.

(I know all this.)

. . . planned takeover of the Germans who own
Thames Water, naturally, and we've just bought up a
fine-looking concern in the Netherlands, and massive
market opportunities coming up with the Chinese and
Indian water business, he says.

(I know all this too.)

Which is why, ah, ah, he says.

Imogen, I say.

Which is why, Imogen, I've brought you down here to
Base Camp, Keith says.

(*This* is Base Camp? Milton Keynes?)

. . . putting you in charge of Pure DND, Keith says.

(Me! In charge of something!)

(Oh my God!)

Thanks, Keith, I say. What's, uh – what exactly is – ?

With your natural tact, he is saying. With your way
with words. With your natural instinctual caring talent
for turning an argument on its head. With your understanding of the politics of locale. With your ability to
deal with media issues head-on. Most of all, with your
style. And I'm the first to admit that right now we need

a woman's touch on the team, ah, ah. We need that more
than anything, and at Pure we will reward more than
anything your ability to look good, look right, say the
right thing, on camera if necessary, under all pressures,
and to take the flak like a man if anything goes pear-
shaped.

(Keith thinks I'm overweight.)

We've stopped outside a prefab identical to all the
others. Keith presses the code-buttons on a door and
lets it swing open. He stands back, gestures to me to
look inside.

There's a new desk, a new computer set-up, a new
chair, a new phone, a new sofa, a shining pot plant.

Pure Dominant Narrative Department, he says.
Welcome home.

Pure — ? I say.

Do I have to carry you over the threshold? he says.
Go on! Take a seat at the desk! It's your seat! It was
purchased for you! Go on!

I don't move from the door. Keith strides in, pulls the
swivel chair out from behind the desk and sends it
rolling towards me. I catch it.

Sit, he says.

I sit in it, in the doorway.

Keith comes over, takes the back of the chair, swivels it round and stands behind me

(which reminds me of what the boy used to do when we went to the shows at the Bught, on the waltzers, the boy who'd hold the back of the waltzer if there were girls in it then make us all laugh like lunatics by giving it an especially dizzying spin.)

Keith's head is by my head. He is speaking into my right ear.

Your first brief, Keith is saying, is a piece replying to the article in the British-based Independent newspaper this morning, which you'll have seen –

(I haven't. Oh God.)

– about how bottled water uses much less stringent testing than tap water. DDR, ah, ah.

DD . . .? I say.

Deny Disparage Rephrase, Keith says. Use your initiative. Your imagination. So many of those so-called regulated tests on tap water useless and some of them actually harmful. Science insists, and many scientists insist. Statistics say. *Our* independent findings versus *their* crackpot findings. You pen it, we place it.

(He wants me to do – what?)

Your second brief is a little tougher. But I know you'll meet it. Small body of irate ethnics in one of our Indian sub-interests factioning against our planned filter-dam two-thirds completed and soon to power four Pure labs in the area. *They say*: our dam blocks their access to fresh water and ruins their crops. *We say*: they're ethnic troublemakers who are trying to involve us in a despicable religious war. Use the word terrorism if necessary. Got it?

(Do what?)

(This chair feels unsafe. Its slight moving under Keith's arm is making me feel sick.)

Fifty-five and upwards per annum, Keith says, nego-tiable after the handling of these first two briefs.

(But it's – wrong.)

Our kind of person, Keith says.

(Keith's midriff is close to my eyes. I can see that his trousers are repressing an erection. More, I can see that he wants me to see it. He is actually showing me his hidden hard-on.)

. . . brightest star in the UK-based Pure-concern sky, he's saying, and I know you can do it, ah, ah, –

(I try to say my name. But I can't speak. My mouth's too dry.)

(It's possible that he came all the way out here to this prefab and set the height level of this chair at the exact height for me to see his erection properly.)

. . . only girl this high in management, he is saying.

(I can't say anything.)

(Then I remember the last time I needed a glass of water.)

(I think about what a glass of water means.)

I can't do this, I say.

Yes you can, he says. You're not a silly girl.

No, I'm not, I say. And I can't make up rubbish and pretend it's true. Those people in India. That water is their right.

Not so, my little Scotty dog, Keith says. According to the World Water Forum 2000, whose subject was water's exact designation, water is not a human right. Water is a human need. And that means we can market it. We can sell a need. It's our *human right* to.

Keith, that's ridiculous, I say. Those words you just used are all in the wrong places.

Keith spins the chair round with me in it until it's facing him. He stands with his hands on the arms and leans over me so I can't get out of the chair. He looks at me solemnly. He gives the chair a playful little warning jolt.

I shake my head.

It's bullshit, Keith, I say. You can't do that.

It's international-government-ratified, he says. It's law. Whether you think it's bullshit or not. And I can do what I like. And there's nothing you or anyone else can do about it.

Then the law should be changed, I hear myself say. It's a wrong law. And there's a lot I can do about it. What I can do is, I can, uh, I can say as loudly as I possibly can, everywhere that I can, that it shouldn't be happening like this, until as many people hear as it takes to make it not happen.

I hear my own voice get louder and louder. But Keith doesn't move. He doesn't flinch. He holds the chair square.

Your surname again? he says quietly.

I take a breath.

It's Gunn, I say.

He shakes his head as if it was him who named me, as if he can decide what I'm called and what I'm not.

Not really Pure material, he says. Pity. You looked just right.

I can feel something rising in me as big as his hard-on. It's anger.

It forces me up on to my feet, lurches me forward in the chair so that my head nearly hits his head and he has to step back.

I take a deep breath. I keep myself calm. I speak quietly.

Which way's the station from here, Keith, and will I need a cab? I ask.

Locked in the ladies toilet in the main prefab while I'm waiting for the taxi, I throw up. Luckily I am adept at throwing up, so I get none of it on my clothes.

(But it is the second time for months and months, I realise as the taxi pulls away from Pure Base Camp, that I haven't thrown up on purpose.)

I get myself back to London. I love London! I walk between Euston and King's Cross like it's some-thing I do all the time, like I belong among all these other people walking along a London street.

I manage to get a seat in a sitting-up carriage on the last sleeper north.

On the journey I tell the other three people in the carriage about Pure and about the people in India.

English people are just as shy and polite as Scottish people really, under all that pretend confidence, and some of them can be very nice.

But I will also have to find a way of telling the story that doesn't make people look away, or go and sit somewhere else.

Still, even though I'm sitting here near-shouting about the ways of the world at a few strangers in a near-empty railway carriage, I feel – what is it I feel?

I feel completely sane.

I feel all energised. I feel so energised on this slow-moving train that it's like I'm travelling faster than the train is. I feel all loaded. A loaded Gunn!

Somewhere in Northumberland, as the train slows up again, I remember the story about the clan I get my name from, the story about the Gunn girl who was wooed by the chief of another clan and who didn't like him. She refused to marry him.

So he came to the Gunn castle one day and he killed all the Gunns he could find, in fact he killed everybody, family or not, that he happened to meet on his way to her chamber. When he got there he broke the door down. He took her by force.

He drove her miles and miles to his own stronghold where he shut her up at the top of a tower until she'd give in.

But she didn't give in. She never gave in. She threw herself out of the tower instead, to her death. Ha!

I used to think that story of my far-back ancestor was a morbid story. But tonight, I mean this morning, on this train about to cross the border between there and here, a story like that one becomes all about where we see it from. Where we're lucky enough

(or unlucky enough)

to see it from.

And listen. Listen, you other two remaining people asleep right now. Listen, world out there, slow-passing beyond the train windows. I'm Imogen Gunn. I come from a family that can't be had. I come from a country that's the opposite of a, what was it, dominant narrative. I'm all Highland adrenalin. I'm all teuchter laughter and I'm all teuchter anger. Pure! Ha!

We roll slowly past the Lowland sea, and the sea belongs to all of us. We roll slowly past the rugged banks of lochs and rivers in a kind of clearness of fine early morning summer light, and they're full of water that belongs to everyone.

Then I think to check my phone.

Seven missed calls – from Paul!

It's a sign!

(And to think I used to think he wasn't the right kind of person for me.)

Even though it's really late, I mean really early morning, I call him straight back without listening to any of the messages.

Paul, I say. It's me. Did I wake you?

No, it's fine, he says. Well, I mean, you did. But Imogen –

Listen, Paul, I say. First there's something I have to say. And it's this. I really like you. I mean, I really, really like you. I've liked you since the very first moment we met. You were at the water cooler. Remember?

Imogen –, he says.

And you know I like you. You know I do. There's that thing between us. You know the thing I mean. The thing where it doesn't matter where you are in a room, you still know exactly where the other person is.

Imogen —, Paul says.

And I know I'm not supposed to say, but I think if you like me too, and if you're not gay or anything, we should do something about it, I say.

Gay? he says.

You know, I say. You never know.

Imogen, have you been drinking? he says.

Just water, I say. And I mean, it's not the same thing at all, I know, but you seem quite female to me, I don't mean that in a bad way, I mean it in a good way, you have a lot of feminine principle, I know that, I know it instinctually, and it's unusual in a man, and I really like it. I love it, actually.

Listen. I've been trying to get hold of you all night, because —, he says.

Yeah, well, if it's about the print-outs, I say, there's no point. The print-outs were irrelevant. I wasn't phoning you about print-outs anyway. I was just trying to get your attention in the only way I could think of without actually telling you I fancied you out loud. And they really don't matter any more, not to me, as I'm no longer a Puree.

It's not the print-outs, Paul says.

And maybe you don't like me, maybe you're embarrassed that I said what I felt, well, never mind, I won't mind, I'm a grown-up, I'll be okay, but I needed to say it out loud, to tell you anyway, and I'm tired of feeling things I never get to express, things that I always have to hold inside, I'm fed up not knowing whether I'm saying the right thing when I do speak, anyway I thought I'd be brave, I thought it was worth it, and I hope you don't mind me saying.

Words are coming out of me like someone turned me on like a tap. It's Paul. He — turns me on!

But as soon as he gets the chance, Paul cuts in.

Imogen. Listen. It's your sister, he says.

My heart in me. Nothing else. Everything else blank.

What about my sister? What's happened to my sister? I say.

★   ★   ★

Paul is waiting for me at the station when the train
pulls in.

Why aren't you at work? I say.

Because I'm here instead, he says.

He slings my bag into the boot of his car then locks
the car with his key fob.

We'll walk, he says. You'll see it better that way. The
first one is on the wall of the Eastgate Centre, I think
because of the traffic coming into town, the people in
cars get long enough to read it when they stop at the
traffic lights. God knows how anybody got up that high
and stayed up there without being disturbed long
enough to do it.

He walks me past Marks and Spencers, about fifteen
yards down the road. Sure enough, the people in the
cars stopped at the traffic lights are peering at something above my head, even leaning out of their car
windows to see it more clearly.

I turn round.

Behind me and above me on the wall the words are
bright, red, huge. They're in the same writing as was
on the Pure sign before they replaced it. They've
been framed in a beautiful, baroque-looking, trompe

l'œil picture-frame in gold. They say: ACROSS THE
WORLD, TWO MILLION GIRLS, KILLED
BEFORE BIRTH OR AT BIRTH BECAUSE THEY
WEREN'T BOYS. THAT'S ON RECORD. ADD
TO THAT THE OFF-RECORD ESTIMATE OF
FIFTY-EIGHT MILLION MORE GIRLS, KILLED
BECAUSE THEY WEREN'T BOYS. THAT'S
SIXTY MILLION GIRLS. Underneath this, in a hand-
writing I recognise, even though it's a lot bigger than
usual: THIS MUST CHANGE. Iphis and Ianthe   the
message girls   2007.

Dear God, I say.

I know, Paul says.

So many girls, I say in case Paul isn't understanding
me.

Yes, Paul says.

Sixty million. I say. How? How can that happen in
this day and age? How do we not know about that?

We do now, he says. Pretty much the whole of
Inverness knows about it now, if they want to. And
more. Much more.

What else? I say.

He walks me back past the shops and up the

pedestrian precinct into town, to the Town House. A small group of people is watching two men in overalls scouring the red off the front wall with a spray gun. IN NO COUNTRY IN THE WORLD RIGHT NOW ARE WOMEN'S WAGES EQUAL TO MEN'S WAGES. THIS MUST CHA

Half the frame and the bit with the names and the date have been sprayed nearly away but are still visible. It's all still legible.

That'll take some shifting, I say.

Paul leads me round the Town House, where a whole side wall is bright red words inside gold. ALL ACROSS THE WORLD, WHERE WOMEN ARE DOING EXACTLY THE SAME WORK AS MEN, THEY'RE BEING PAID BETWEEN THIRTY TO FORTY PERCENT LESS. THAT'S NOT FAIR. THIS MUST CHANGE. Iphis and Ianthe   the message boys   2007.

Probably Catholics, a woman says. It's disgusting.

Aye, it'll fair ruin the tourism, another says. Who'd be wanting to come and see the town if the town's covered in this kind of thing? Nobody.

And we can say goodbye to winning that Britain in Bloom this year now, her friend says.

And to Antiques Roadshow ever coming back to Inverness and all, another says.

It's a scandal! another is saying. Thirty to forty percent!

Aye well, a man next to her says. It's no fair, right enough, if that's true, what it says there.

Aye, but why would *boys* write *that* kind of thing on a building? a woman is saying. It's not natural.

Too right they should, the scandal-woman says. And would you not have thought we were equal now, here, after all that stravaiging in the seventies and the eighties?

Aye, but we're equal here, in Inverness, the first woman says.

In your dreams we're equal, the scandal-woman says.

Nevertheless, equal or no, it's no reason to paint it all over the Town House, the woman's friend says.

The scandal-woman is arguing back as we walk up round the side of the Castle. In gilted red on the front wall above the Castle door it says in a jolly arc, like the name of a house painted right above its threshold, that only one percent of the world's assets are held by women. Iphis and Ianthe the message girls 2007.

From here we can see right across the river that there are huge red words on the side of the cathedral too. I can't see what they say, but I can make out the red.

Two million girls annually forced into marriage worldwide, Paul says seeing me straining to make it out. And on Eden Court Theatre, on the glass doors, it says that sexual or domestic violence affects one out of every three women and girls worldwide and that this is the world's leading cause of injury and death for women.

I can make out the *this must change* from here, I say.

We lean on the Castle railing and Paul lists the other places that have been written on, what the writing says, and about how the police phoned Pure for me.

Your sister and her friend are both in custody up at Raigmore, he says.

Robin's not her friend, I say. Robin's her other half.

Right, Paul says. I'll run you up there now. You'll need to arrange bail. I did try. My bank wouldn't let me.

Hang on, I say. I bet you anything –

What? he says.

I bet you their double bail there's a message some-where on Flora too, I say.

I can't afford it, he shouts behind me.

I run down to the statue of Flora MacDonald shielding her eyes, watching for Bonnie Prince Charlie, still dressed in the girls' clothes she lent him for his escape from the English forces, to come sailing back to her all the way up the River Ness.

I walk round the statue three times reading the words ringing the base of her. Tiny, clear, red, a couple of centimetres high: WOMEN OCCUPY TWO PERCENT OF SENIOR MANAGEMENT POSITIONS IN BUSINESS WORLDWIDE. THREE AND A HALF PERCENT OF THE WORLD'S TOTAL NUMBER OF CABINET MINISTERS ARE WOMEN. WOMEN HAVE NO MINISTERIAL POSITIONS IN NINETY-THREE COUNTRIES OF THE WORLD. THIS MUST CHANGE. Iphis and Ianthe   the message boys   2007.

Good old Flora. I pat her base.

Paul catches me up.

I'll nip down and get the car and pick you up here, he says, and we'll head up the hill –

Take me home first, I say. I need a bath. I need some breakfast. Then maybe you and me can have a talk. Then I'll take us up to the police station on my Rebel.

On your what? But we should really go up to the station right now, Imogen, he says. It's been all night.

Are you not wanting to talk to me, then? I say.

Well, I do, actually, he says, I've got a lot to say, but do you not think we should –

I shake my head.

I think the message boy-girls'll be proud to be in there, I say.

Oh, he says. I never thought of it that way.

Let's leave the police on message until lunchtime, I say. Then we'll go up and sort the bail. And after that we'll all go for something to eat.

Paul is very good in bed.

(Thank goodness.)

(Well, I knew he would be.)

(Well, I hoped.)

I feel met by you, he says afterwards. It's weird.

(That's exactly what it feels like. I felt met by him the first time I saw him. I felt met by him all the times we weren't even able to meet each other's eyes.)

I definitely felt met by you this morning at the station, I say.

Ha, he says. That's funny.

We both laugh like idiots.

It is the loveliest laughing ever.

(I feel like we should always be meeting each other off trains, I think inside my head. That's if we're not actually on the same train, going the same way.)

I say it out loud.

I feel like we should always be meeting each other off trains, that's if we're not actually on the same train travelling together. Or am I saying too much out loud? I say.

You're saying it too quietly, he says. I wish you'd shout it.

It's raining quite heavily when we make love again and afterwards I can hear the rhythmic drip, heavy and steady, from the place above the window where the drainpipe is blocked. The rhythm of it goes against, and at the same time makes a kind of sense of, the randomness of the rain happening all round it.

I never knew how much I liked rain till now.

When Paul goes downstairs to make coffee I remember myself. I go to the bathroom. I catch sight of my own face in the little mirror.

ALI SMITH

I go through to Anthea's room where the big mirror is. I sit on the edge of her bed and I make myself look hard at myself.

I am a lot less than an 8 now.

(I can see bones here, here, here, here and here.)

(Is that good?)

Back in my own room I see my clothes on the chair. I remember the empty clothes on that memorial, made to look soft, but made of metal.

(I have thought for a long time that the way my clothes hang on me is more important than me inside them.)

I hear Paul moving about in the bathroom. He turns on the shower.

He turns everything in the world on, not just me. Ha ha.

I like the idea of Paul in my shower. The shower, for some reason, has been where I've done my thinking and my asking since I was teenage. I've been standing those few minutes in the shower every day for God knows how long now, talking to nothing like we used to do when we were small, Anthea and I, and knelt by the sides of our beds.

(Please make me the correct size. The correct shape.
The right kind of daughter. The right kind of sister.
Someone who isn't fazed or sad. Someone whose family
has held together, not fallen apart. Someone who simply
feels *better*. Please make things better. THIS MUST
CHANGE.)

I get up. I call the police station.

The man on the desk is unbelievably informal.

Oh aye, he says. Now, is it one of the message girls
or boys or whatever, or one of the seven dwarves that
you're after? Which one would you like? We've got
Dopey, Sneezy, Grumpy, Bashful, Sleepy, Eye-fist, and
another one whose name I'd have to look up for you.

I'd like to talk to my sister, Anthea Gunn, please, I say.
And that's enough flippancy about their tag from you.

About their what, now? he says.

Years from now, I say, you and the Inverness
Constabulary will be nothing but a list of dry dusty
names locked in an old computer memory stick. But the
message girls, the message boys. They'll be legend.

Uh huh, he says. Well, if you'd like to hang up your
phone now, Ms Gunn, I'll have your wee sister call you
back in a jiffy.

(I consider making a formal complaint, while I wait for the phone to go. *I am the only person permitted to make fun of my sister.*)

Where've you been? she says when I answer.

Anthea, do you really think you'll change the world a single jot by calling yourself by a funny name and doing what you've been doing? You really think you'll make a single bit of difference to all the unfair things and all the suffering and all the injustice and all the hardship with a few words?

Yes, she says.

Okay. Good, I say.

Good? she says. Aren't you angry? Aren't you really furious with me?

No, I say.

No? she says. Are you lying?

But I think you're going to have to get a bit better at dodging the police, I say.

Yeah, she says. Well. We're working on it.

You and the girl with the little wings coming out of her heels, I say.

Are you being rude about Robin? she says. Because if you are, I'll make fun of your motorbike again.

Ha ha, I say. You can borrow one of my crash
helmets if you want. But you might not want to, since
there's no wings on it like there are on Robin's helmet.

Eh? she says.

It's a reference, I say. To a source.

Eh? she says.

Don't say eh, say pardon or excuse me. I mean like
Mercury.

Like what? she says.

Mercury, I say. *You* know. Original message boy.
Wings on his heels. Wait a minute, I'll go downstairs
and get my Dictionary of Mythical —

No, no, Midge, don't go anywhere. Just listen, she
says. I've not got long on this phone. I can't ask Dad.
There's no one Robin can ask. Just help us out this
once. Please. I won't ask again.

I know. You must be desperate to get out of that
kilt, I say and I crack up laughing again.

Well, when you stop finding yourself so hilarious, she
says, actually, if you *could* bring me a change of clothes
that'd be great.

But you've been okay, you're both okay up there? I say.

We're good. But if you could, like I say, just, eh,

quite urgently, justify half an hour's absence to
Dominorm or whoever, and disengage yourself from the
Pure empire long enough to come and bail us out. I'll
pay you back. I promise.

You'll need to, I say. I'm unemployed now.

Eh? she says.

I'm disengaged, I say. I'm no longer Pure.

No! she says. What happened? What's wrong?

Nothing and everything is what happened, I say. And
at Pure, everything's wrong. Everything in the world.
But you know this already.

Seriously? she says.

Honest to goodness, I say.

Wow, she says. When did it happen?

What? I say.

The miracle. The celestial exchange of my sister for
you, whoever you are.

A glass of water given in kindness, that's what did it,
I say.

Eh? she says.

Stop saying eh, I say. Anyway I thought we'd saunter
on up in a wee while –

Eh, can I just stress the word urgent? she says.

Though I thought I might drive out to a garden centre first and buy some seeds and bulbs –

Urgent urgent urgent urgent, she says.

And then I thought I might spend the rest of the afternoon and early evening down on the river bank –

URGENT, she yells down the phone.

– planting a good slogan or two that'll appear mysteriously in the grass of it next spring. RAIN BELONGS TO EVERYONE. Or THERE'S NO SUCH THING AS A SECOND SEX. Or PURE DEAD = BRILLIANT. Something like that.

Oh. That's such a good idea, she says. Planting in the riverbank. That's such a fantastic idea.

Also, you're being too longwinded, I say. All the long sentences. It needs to be simpler. You need sloganeering help. You definitely need some creative help –

Does that creative have a small c or a big C? she says.

– and did you know, by the way, since we're talking sloganeering, I say –

Midge, just come and help, she says. Like, now. And don't forget to bring the clothes.

– that the word slogan, I say, comes from the Gaelic? It's a word with a really interesting history –

No, no, no, she says, please don't start with all that correct-word-saying-it-properly-the-right-way-not-the-wrong-way stuff right now, just come up and get us out of here, Midge, yes? Midge? Are you there?

(Ha-ha!)

What's the magic word? I say.

all together now

Reader, I married him/her.

It's the happy ending. Lo and behold.

I don't mean we had a civil ceremony. I don't mean we had a civil partnership. I mean we did what's still impossible after all these centuries. I mean we did the still-miraculous, in this day and age. I mean we got married. I mean we here came the bride. I mean we walked down the aisle. I mean we step we gailied, on we went, we Mendelssohned, we epithalamioned, we raised high the roofbeams, carpenters, for there was no other bride, o bridegroom, like her. We crowned each other with the garlands of flowers. We stamped on the wineglasses wrapped in the linen. We jumped the broomstick. We lit the candles. We crossed the sticks. We circled the table. We circled each other. We fed each other the honey and the walnuts from the silver spoons; we fed each other the tea and the sake and we sweetened the tea for each other; we fed each other the borhani beneath the pretty cloth; we fed each other a taste of lemon, vinegar, cayenne and honey, one for each of the four elements. We handfasted, then we asked for the blessing of the air, the fire, the water and the earth; we tied the knot with grass, with ribbon, with silver rope, with a string of shells; we poured water on the ground in the four directions of the wind and we called on the presence of our ancestors as witnesses, so may it be! We gave each other the kola nuts to symbolise commitment, the eggs and the dates and the chestnuts to symbolise righteousness, plenty, fertility, the thirteen gold coins to symbolise constant unselfishness. With these rings we us wedded.

What I mean is. There, under the trees, on a fresh spring day by the banks of the River Ness, that fast black backbone of a Scottish northern town; there, flanked by presbyterian church after presbyterian church, we gave our hands in marriage under the blossom, gave each other and took each other for better, for worse, in sickness or health, to love, comfort, honour, cherish, protect, and to have and to hold each other from that day forward, for as long as we both should live till death us would part.

Ness I said Ness I will Ness.

Into thin air, to the nothing that was there, with the river our witness, we said yes. We said we did. We said we would.

We'd thought we were alone, Robin and I. We'd thought it was just us, under the trees outside the cathedral. But as soon as we'd made our vows there was a great whoop of joy behind us, and when we turned round we saw all the people, there must have been hundreds, they were clapping and cheering, they were throwing confetti, they waved and they roared celebration.

My sister was there at the front with her other half, Paul. She was happy. She smiled. Paul looked happy. He was growing his hair. My sister gestured to me like she couldn't believe it, at a couple standing not far from her — look! — was it them? — sure enough, it *was* them, our father and our mother, both, and they were standing together and they weren't arguing, they were talking to each other very civilly, they clinked their glasses as I watched.

They're discussing the unsuitability of the wedding, Midge said.

I nodded. First time they've agreed on anything in years, I said.

All the people from the rest of the tale were there too; Becky from Reception; the two work experience girls, Chantelle and her friend Lorraine; Brian, who was going out with Chantelle; and Chantelle's mum, who wasn't in the story as such but who'd clearly also taken a shine to Brian; a whole gaggle of Pure people, including the security men who first arrested Robin; they waved and smiled. Not Norman or Dominic, were those their names? they'd been promoted to Base Camp, so they weren't there, at least not that I saw, and not the boss of bosses, Keith, I don't remember seeing him either. But the whole of the Provost's office came, and some officials from other places we'd written on; the theatre, the shopping mall, the Castle. A male-voice choir from the Inverness Police Force attended, they sang a beautiful arrangement of songs from Gilbert and Sullivan. Then the Inverness Constabulary female-voice choir sang an equally beautiful choral arrangement of Don't Cha (Wish Your Girlfriend Was Hot Like Me). Then the Provost made an eloquent speech. Inverness, she said, once famed for its faith in unexpected ancient creatures of the deep, had now become famous for something new: for fairness, for art, and for the art of fairness. Inverness, now world-renowned for its humane and galvanising public works of art, had quadrupled its tourist intake. Thousands more people were coming especially to view the public exhibits. And not just Antiques Roadshow, but Songs of Praise, Question Time, Newsnight Review and several other tv programmes had *all* petitioned the council, keen to record themselves in front of the famous sloganned walls. The Inverness art may have spawned copycat art in other cities and towns, she said, but none so good as in the city whose new defining motto, inscribed on all the signposts at all the entrypoints to the city, would be from this day forth *A Hundred Thousand Welcomes And When You See A Wrong, Write It! Ceud Mile Failte! Còir! Sgriobh!*

Really terrible slogan, I said privately to Robin.

Your sister thought it up, Robin said. Definitely in line for a job as Council Creative.

Which is your family? I asked Robin. She pointed them out. They were by the drinks table with Venus,

Artemis and Dionysos; her father and mother were
cuddling the baby Cupid, which was problematic
because of the arrows (in fact there was a bit of a
fuss later when Lorraine cut her finger open on an
arrow-tip, and even more problems when Artemis
and Chantelle were found down the riverbank in the
dusk light firing arrows at the rabbits on the grass
at the side of the Castle and, Chantelle being very
short-sighted, the damage to four passing cars had
to be paid for, and Brian had to be comforted after
Chantelle swore eternal celibacy, so it was lucky
that Chantelle's mum had come with her after
all).

Then we had the speeches, and Midge read out
the apologies, including one from the Loch Ness
Monster, who'd sent us an old rusty underwater radar
scanner, some signed photos of herself and a lovely
set of silver fishknives, and there was a half gold-edged,
half black-edged telegram-poem from John Knox,
sorry he couldn't make it to be there with us even in
spirit:

Here's tae ye,
Wha's like ye?
Far too many
And ye're all damnt to Hell.
But whit can I say,
It's a weddin day,
So come on, raise your glasses now,
And wish the damnt pair weel!

We had the blessings then, and the toasts. Honour, riches, marriage-blessing, Love, continuance, and increasing, Hourly joys be still upon us, Juno sing her blessings on us, till all the seas gang dry, my dear, and the rocks melt wi' the sun. May our eternal summer never fade. May the road rise up to meet us, and may God always hold us in the palm of His hand. A dog on two legs was drinking too much whisky. A goddess so regal she must have been Isis spent the whole reception making fine new guests out of clay. A beautiful Greek couple came graciously up and shook our hands; they were newlyweds themselves, they said, and how had the run-up to the wedding been? was it as nervewracking as

it'd been for them? They'd never thought they'd make
it. But they had, they were happy, and they wished us
all happiness. They told us to honeymoon in Crete,
where their families would make us welcome, and that's
exactly what we did, Robin and I, when the wedding
was over, we hotfooted it to the hot island, its surfaces
layered with wild flowers, marjoram, sage and thyme,
its rocks split by the force of tiny white and pink and
yellow flowers and everywhere the scent of herbs and
salt and sea. We stood where the Iphis story had origi-
nated, we stood between red-painted pillars in the
reconstructed palace, we went to the museum to see the
ancient, pieced-together, re-imagined painting of the
athlete, the acrobat, boy or girl or both, who was agile
enough to somersault right over the top of the back of
the charging bull. We stood where the civilised, rich,
cultured, Minoan cannibals had lived before nature had
simply flooded them into oblivion, and we thought
about the story that arose from their rituals, the story
of the annual sacrifice of the seven boys and seven girls
to the bull-headed beast, and the clever artist, the man
who invented human wings, who devised the girls and
the boys a safe way out of the bloody maze.

But back at the wedding the band had struck up now, and what a grand noise, for the legendary red-faced fiddler who played at all the best weddings had come, and had had a drink, and had got out his fiddle, he was the man to turn curved wood and horsehair, cat-gut and resin into a single blackbird then into a flight of black-birds singing all the evenings at once, then into a spawn of happy salmon, into the return of the longed-for boat to a port, into the longing that waits in a lucky place for two people who don't yet know each other to meet exactly there, where the stones grass over, the borders cross themselves. It was the song of the flow of things, the song of the undammed river, and there with the fiddler was his sidekick, who doubled the tune and who, when he played alongside his partner, found in every-thing he laid hands on (whistle, squeezebox, harp, guitar, old empty oilcan and a stick or stone to bang it with) the kind of music that not only made the bushes and the trees pull themselves out of the ground and move where they could hear better, but made them throw their leaves and twigs up in the air, made all the seagulls clap their wings, made all the dogs of the Highlands bark with joy, made all the roofs dance on the houses, made every paving stone of the whole town tear itself up, stand itself on its pointed corner and do a happy pirouette, even made the old cathedral itself on its fixed foundations leap and caper.

Up the river it came, then, the astonishing little boat, up the river that no boats ever came up, with its two great fibreglass juts like the horns of a goat or a cow or a goddess held ahead of it, and its sail full and white against the trees and the sky. How it got from the loch through the Islands, how it did the impossible, got under the Infirmary Bridge with that full huge sail up we'll never know, but it did, it sailed the stretch of Ness Bank and it docked right below us, and there at the wheel was our grandmother, and throwing the rope to be caught was our grandfather. Robert and Helen Gunn, they were back from the sea, in time for the party.

We felt in our water that something was happening! our grandmother called up to us as she put her foot on dry land. We wouldn't miss this, no, not for the world!

Well, girls, and have you been good, and has the world been good to you? and how was your catch? have you landed fine fish? that was our grandfather, his old arms round us, him ruffling our hair.

They were younger than the day they left. They were brown and robust, their faces and hands were lined like the trunks of trees. They met Robin. They met Paul. They flung their arms round them like family.

Our grandmother danced the Canadian Barn Dance with Paul.

Our grandfather danced the Gay Gordons with Robin.

The music and the dancing went on late into the night. In fact, there was still dancing going on when the night was over, the light coming back and the new day dawning.

Uh-huh. Okay. I know.

In my dreams.

What I mean is, we stood on the bank of the river under the trees, the pair of us, and we promised the nothing that was there, the nothing that made us, the nothing that was listening, that we truly desired to go beyond our selves.

And that's the message. That's it. That's all.

Rings that widen on the surface of a loch above a thrown-in stone. A drink of water offered to a thirsty traveller on the road. Nothing more than what happens when things come together, when hydrogen, say, meets oxygen, or a story from then meets a story from now, or stone meets water meets girl meets boy meets bird meets hand meets wing meets bone meets light meets dark meets eye meets word meets world meets grain of sand meets thirst meets hunger meets need meets dream meets real meets same meets different meets death meets life meets end meets beginning all over again, the story of nature itself, ever-inventive, making one thing out of another, and one thing into another, and nothing lasts, and nothing's lost, and nothing ever perishes, and things can always change, because things will always change, and things will always be different, because things can always be different.

And it was always the stories that needed the telling that gave us the rope we could cross any river with. They balanced us high above any crevasse. They made us be natural acrobats. They made us be brave. They met us well. They changed us. It was in their nature to.

And there's always a whole other kittle of fish, our

grandfather said in my ear as he reached down and tucked the warm stone into my hand, there it was, ready for me to throw.

Right, Anthea?

Right, Grandad, I said.

Acknowledgements and thanks

I've adapted the story of Burning Lily from the account of the early life of Lilian Lenton in *Rebel Girls* by Jill Liddington (Virago, 2006).

The myth of Iphis originates in Book 9 of Ovid's *Metamorphoses*. 'Carry your gifts to the temples, happy pair, and rejoice, confident and unafraid!' It is one of the cheeriest metamorphoses in the whole work, one of the most happily resolved of its stories about the desire for and the ramifications of change.

The statistics in chapter four were collated by Womankind (www.womankind.org.uk), a UK charity whose raison d'être is to provide voice, aid and rights to disempowered women worldwide.

I've borrowed the rhetorical structure of one of Keith's talks from a paper given in 2001 by the sociologist

J-P Joseph about the global water corporation Vivendi Universal, quoted in *Blue Gold* by Maude Barlow and Tony Clarke (Earthscan, 2002). The writings of Vandana Shiva are another good place to help comprehend what's happening right now, worldwide, when it comes to the politics of water, as is *H20: A Biography of Water* by Philip Ball (Weidenfeld & Nicolson, 1999), which lets us know, among many other marvellous things, that 'water is bent'.

Thank you, Xandra. Thank you, Jeanette.
Thank you, Rachel, Bridget and Kasia.
Thank you, Robyn and Hiraani at This ASFC.
Thank you, Andrew, and everyone at Wylie's, especially Tracy. Thank you, Anya.

Thank you, Lucy.

Thank you, Sarah.

Also available in the Canongate Myths Series

THE PENELOPIAD

MARGARET ATWOOD

In Homer's *Odyssey*, Penelope is portrayed as the quintessential faithful wife, her story a salutary lesson through the ages. In a splendid contemporary twist to the ancient tale, Margaret Atwood has chosen to give the telling of it to Penelope herself, answering the question: 'What was she *really* up to?'

'Penelope flies with the help of the sardonic, deadpan voice Atwood lends her, a tone half-Dorothy Parker, half-*Desperate Housewives*.' Boyd Tonkin, *Independent*

'An exquisitely poised book.' Lucy Hughes-Hallett, *Sunday Times*

£7.99

ISBN 978 1 84195 704 3

WEIGHT

JEANETTE WINTERSON

In ancient Greek mythology, Atlas leads a rebellion against the Olympians, incurring divine wrath. He is condemned to shoulder the world forever; but when the hero Heracles is tasked with stealing the golden apples of life, he strikes a bargain with Atlas and an uneasy partnership between the two defiant men is born. With her typical wit and verve, Jeanette Winterson brings Atlas into the twenty-first century, turning the familiar on its head in a dazzling new tale.

'A touching meditation on the difficult journey to self-knowledge, and also extremely funny.' Lucasta Miller, *Guardian*

£6.99

ISBN 978 1 84195 775 3